Trompe l'Oeil

BEAUTY AND THE BEAST RETOLD

BETHANY KOHLER

PASSERIDAE PRESS

ISBN: 979-8-9860532-1-9 (paperback)
ISBN: 979-8-9860532-0-2 (e-book)

This is a work of fiction. Names, characters, places, and events are products of the author's imagination.

Book design by Bethany Kohler
Cover art by Jordan Kohler

Printed in the United States of America

Preface

The history of oral tradition is something I have always found fascinating. I can imagine how it might have been, before literacy was widespread. Ballads being memorized and repeated; tales being told and retold. Grandparents telling stories to the children, which had been told to them when they were children themselves. Stories were alive—never written in a book, but passed down from generation to generation nonetheless.

One of the beautiful things about folklore in the days of oral tradition was that each storyteller had the freedom to tell the story their own way, with their own spin, while still following the outlined plot and including all the key elements. The following is my version—with my own twist —of an old and beloved folktale, most commonly known as: 'The Beauty and The Beast'.

As far as I know, the earliest written version of this story was the work of Gabrielle-Suzanne Barbot de Villeneuve in 1740. Some readers may be familiar with Lang's or Beaumont's abridged versions of Villeneuve's work, and may recognize my inspiration. However, Villeneuve herself was only writing her own version of an existing tale. Research recently coming out of Durham University and the New University of Lisbon suggests that the true origins of the folktale date back through many hundreds of years of oral tradition.

So here I am, adding my piece to the lore, carrying on the long tradition—though mine be written down.

Trompe l'Oeil

First Chapter

Once upon a time, in a large and bustling port city called Florens, there lived a wealthy merchant. His was among the chief houses in one of the chief streets in the most fashionable district of the city. In it with him lived his four children, one son and three daughters. Sorrow had visited his house when his youngest was yet a child; his wife had fallen ill and met an untimely death. After the first shock and grief of her passing, the merchant had learned to find consolation in his children, and distraction in his work, and lived a happy and busy life.

Although the merchant tried not to have favorites among his children, he could not help but look with especial fondness upon the youngest, for she so reminded him of his beloved wife. Even as a young girl, she had a natural grace of movement, made particularly potent and endearing by her being completely unconscious of it.

The two elder daughters were quite popular in their social circle, being admired for their beauty and charm. Their brother was likewise well-favored, and had many friends. When the time came for the youngest daughter's "coming out," Society was eager to pass its judgment. Would she live up to her name? Would she outshine her sisters? By a whim of her mother, the youngest had been named Beauty, so expectation was high in her favor.

For one whole week she was considered quite the prettiest of the Duveau family. But after another week, Society's infatuation began to fade. She was not really any more beautiful than her sisters. Estella and Mariette were charming and clever, as well as pretty. Beauty was too blunt. She did not possess the art of tactful conversation, and Society did not approve.

Beauty was unlike her sisters in her interests as well as her manners. Estella and Mariette delighted in silks and lace, and the minutiae of Fashion. Beauty enjoyed wearing pretty things, but it did not consume her interest the same way. She preferred the natural and wild aesthetic, delighting in a cloudy sky, or an apple tree in blossom, or the rugged crags that dropped off into the sea. Her sisters were regular attendees at the theater and concert hall, for such was fashionable. Beauty sometimes joined them, but the press of people was a deterrent. She preferred sitting alone, listening to the ocean's rhythmic music, or when the song of a nightingale came through her window on a warm summer evening.

Thus, Society passed its final judgment: the youngest Duveau girl was "withdrawn" and "unsociable." Wasn't it a pity.

Mssr. Duveau delighted in gratifying his children's every wish. His daughters were provided with music lessons, dance lessons, riding lessons, tutors in Greek and Italian, and any other subject to which they took a fancy. As for the classical subjects, the girls were left to study or not as they chose.

Beauty was fascinated by languages, and enjoyed her Greek as much as her spinet lessons. Books were to her like inviting doorways into far away lands, or goldmines of information, inspiring thoughts she would never have explored on her own. She had a mind which desired to know the mechanisms behind things, and the cause of any given outcome. This natural curiosity led her to study the sciences, and dabble in philosophy, so that even left to her own devices, her education was fairly well rounded.

Estella and Mariette, on the other hand, found such studies unutterably dull. They studied their Italian with some dedication, but only because it was fashionable to drop little *frasi Italiane* in everyday conversation. They could see no purpose in the endless monotony of Greek, and declared that Philosophy was incomprehensible rubbish. As they were permitted—even encouraged—by their father to study only what interested or pleased them, they soon gave up their Greek, along with any serious study of the classical subjects.

Their father never considered that this would spoil them, for his only thought was to bring them happiness and comfort. He loved them so much that he would have spared them all pain, were it in his power. Whether or not that was wise, time proved it beyond his ability.

The summer of Beauty's eighteenth year was an eventful one in the Duveau household. All that spring Estella had received the marked attentions of Sir Roger

Lambert. She had encouraged these attentions "tactfully," as she herself said, and as spring gave way to summer, a courtship blossomed.

Edmund returned home from his first year at university, bringing with him several new acquaintances to spend part of their holiday by the seashore. For nearly a month the house was fair bursting at the seams. Excursions and picnics were planned and executed, and the loud voices and boisterous laughter of young men, who were still mostly boys, filled the house.

Mariette had a growing string of beaus, for she had a natural quick wit in conversation, and flirted with almost any young man she came across. She was a creature ruled by her emotions, and so was rather changeable, and gave or withheld encouragement as her mood dictated. One day she would favor George Albert, and the next would talk about Leopold as though no one else existed, only to have forgotten them both the day following.

Beauty had very little patience for her sister's immoderate effusions. Once or twice she attempted to bring some levelheadedness to Mariette's outbursts of emotion, but was only met with resentment or ignored. She began to suspect that Mariette really liked herself best, and so those who most flattered her vanity were her favorites.

As for Sir Roger, Beauty couldn't help but wonder what it was Estella saw in him. He didn't seem to think about anything except horse-racing and the latest fashions. The first conversation Beauty ever had with him, the subject had ranged from tailcoats and waistcoats to boots and cravats. Another time, she learned from him that taking a "nip of brandy" before bed was "the thing to do." He stated emphatically that it improved overall health. When Beauty asked how, he waved his hand dismissively and said, "Lawd, I'm not a doctor."

All of this did not win him a very high place in Beauty's estimation. Perhaps it was unfair to judge him after only a few brief conversations. Perhaps there was another side of him that Beauty had not seen. She did try to entertain this idea, but every interaction only worked to cement her original impression.

Around this time, Beauty also noticed a cloud gathering on her father's brow. He spent more and more time consumed by business matters, and although he affected a cheerful attitude at mealtimes, Beauty's keen eye perceived the lines that creased his forehead when he thought there was no one to see. She wondered what could be the cause, and guessed that her father was under some weight of care, but he evaded her questions when she approached the subject. She ventured once to ask how the business was going, and if there was anything she could do. He put forward the feint of cheerfulness and said he was sure everything would sort out, as soon as the ships came in.

So Beauty watched with a subdued manner all the frivolity of her brother and sisters, who went on unaware of any change. And she watched with growing concern as her father shut himself up in his study continually, and she could no longer erase the lines on his brow, as much as she tried.

Businessmen came to see him, and Bankers. Still the ships did not come in. Weeks passed; the end of summer approached. Estella was sure that a proposal was forthcoming. And still the ships did not come in.

Edmund's fellow collegians had returned to their respective homes, and the Duveau house returned to relative tranquility. Edmund turned his attention to study, in preparation for the coming term. Beauty liked to sit with him, perusing a book of her own, while he studied. She preferred this more studious side of her brother to the frivolous lad he became around his friends.

Then one evening the news came: the ships would not be coming in. Every vessel on which Mssr. Duveau had an interest, had encountered either devastating storms or ruthless pirates, and all his goods and investments were irretrievable—destroyed, sunk to the bottom of the sea, or in the hands of marauders.

Beauty now discovered the full extent of the weight her father had been carrying for months. His business had been quietly declining for some time, unnoticed by his children. He had taken out a loan against the wealth that he expected from his ships' cargo, to pay for Edmund's college expenses, and the various parties and new dresses which his daughters required for the social season. The terms of the loan allowed that no interest would be accrued until a certain date, at which time an enormous interest would be incurred and compounded thenceforth. That date had passed, and now Mssr. Duveau owed more than twice over what he had originally borrowed, with no means of repaying except by dissolving his assets.

The full disclosure of this news struck Edmund deeply. He felt that he had been foolish and reckless in his habits, contributing to his father's troubles, and he vowed in his heart to be a better son. He made light of leaving school, telling his father cheerily that he probably would have dropped out anyway; his classes bored him, and he liked working with his hands. Little did he know what sweet balm this was to his father's heavy heart, even though his father suspected the truth.

Mssr. Duveau sold their house in Bolanger Square,

with all the luxuries it entailed, and after discharging his debts, there was very little left. A small farm in the country, where he had fond memories of his wife when they were newly married and had not visited since her death, was the only property that remained to him. He decided to move his family there, though even the thought of the place was bittersweet to him. They would work the land for their livelihood.

This change was a harsh blow to Estella and Mariette. They were not convinced at first that they truly had to leave the city for some obscure provincial farm. They tried turning to their many friends for help, feeling certain that one or another of them would be glad to welcome them until their father "got back on his feet." But those they had once called friends now shunned them, pretended to be away from home when visits were paid, even crossed the street to avoid them, while casting scornful glances over their shoulders.

They realized that they were rejected by the very society they had led. Their suitors likewise disappeared; no dowry and no social status meant they were no longer of any interest. After this discovery, they were almost grateful to be moving so far away from the city and all those they once had known, considering themselves utterly humiliated in the eye of Society.

The final blow for Estella was learning that even Sir Roger had withdrawn his attentions—probably thanking his lucky star that he had not involved himself too deeply and could extricate himself with comparative ease. No proposal had taken place, and now never would; Estella was crushed. She would never love again. Her chance had passed. These were the thoughts with which she soothed her broken heart as she resigned herself to a life of obscurity.

Although Beauty had only a cheerful face for her family during this transition, once or twice her tears flowed at times when there were no witnesses. The velvet cushion in her favorite window nook in the old library, where so many pleasant hours had been spent, was dampened by her grief. And the grass beneath the spreading oak tree in the garden, where so many precious memories of childhood had played out, was watered by her tears.

Her sisters made no attempt to hide their wretchedness, and sobbed openly at the dinner table. It was seeing all her family so saddened that made Beauty hide her own grief. She did not wish to add to their sorrow, especially her father's. So her brave and sweet smile was ready for them on every occasion, and her melancholy was saved for moments of solitude.

In her endeavors to comfort and support her father, Beauty succeeded even more than she knew. A single word spoken in love can mean more than mounds of jewels, and it is sometimes the small things that have the greatest impact.

Though she did not rejoice in their circumstances, it gladdened her heart to be able to share her father's burdens. Before they even left their house in the city, she began devising plans as to how she could run a thrifty household. This office traditionally fell to the eldest daughter, but the thought of Estella taking on such duties never entered any of their heads—least of all Estella's. Such things were not her forte, nor Mariette's, so they naturally and without discussion fell to Beauty.

The journey to their new home was an uneventful one. Three long days were spent on the stagecoach, taking them from Florens to Druane. There, a second coach was hired to carry them to Isole. The common road from Druane to Isole skirted the western borders of Inconnu Forest; for two days the scenery was trees to the east, and trees occasionally broken by fields and meadows to the west.

When they finally arrived in the hamlet of Isole, they were all travel-weary. Five days confined to a coach, although interrupted now and again by spells of walking beside that same coach, made each of them restless and irritable to varying degrees.

They spent a night at the only inn Isole had to offer, and in the morning a wagon took them on the last stage of their journey. For two hours they bumped and jostled along, and Estella and Mariette felt truly that they were outcasts, banished from all nice society. Here among the cows and goats, they would shrivel away, unjustly punished for the wrongs of others. If only their father had not lost their fortune.

Second Chapter

Though harvest was in full swing when they settled into their new home, they had no crops of their own to harvest, as there had been no one to plant them. So Edmund went to neighboring farms to work in their fields as a day-laborer.

Beauty took it upon herself to arrange the house in the most comfortable and homey way possible. Since they could afford but one servant to help with the cooking and cleaning, and her sisters could hardly be prevailed upon to lift a finger, many duties fell to Beauty that she had not the experience to anticipate. But she rose to meet every challenge with a fierce determination.

Her father set himself, with surprising vigor, to making some necessary repairs to the house, which had been shuttered up for many years, before winter set in. And after the house, he would turn his attention to repairing the barn, he said, in preparation to receive livestock.

It had been scarce a week since they arrived at their new home, before Beauty was taxed to the breaking point. She had worked from sunup till sundown, without voicing a single complaint. That morning she had ruined her favorite muslin dress at the washboard—learning by experience how not to wash muslin. She had burnt her hand tending the kitchen fire. Her father came in to supper looking more tired than she had ever seen him look. And Mariette chose that moment to saunter into the room, and begin complaining of their rustic furnishings and simple fare, comparing them to the fashions and luxuries of Florens.

Beauty turned on her with flashing eyes. "Don't you dare criticize what you will not lift a finger to change! You haven't even left Florens—your habits haven't changed. You won't be bothered to do any of the work. You sleep as long as you choose, and laze about as though waiting for invisible servants to attend you. Well there aren't any! Spend an afternoon washing and hanging curtains, and scrubbing and scouring till your back aches, and paring potatoes; then you may complain about the life we left behind."

Mariette stared in amazement. Then she began to whimper. "I'm not like you. You were clearly born for a country life. I wasn't."

Beauty rolled her eyes in exasperation, but made no further reply. The flash of her anger had already subsided to an inward smolder, and she knew any further argument with her sister would be fruitless. She did not feel herself born for a country life in the least. The work was hard, and no matter how much was done, there was always more to do. Did Mariette imagine she preferred scrubbing and scouring to other pursuits? No; she would much prefer curling up in a quiet corner and losing herself in a book. But if she didn't do the work, who would?

After witnessing this outburst, and seeing how little his older daughters contributed to the work of the household, Mssr. Duveau sat them down and spoke to them admonishingly of duty and hardship and sharing the load. After this, they were a little better about helping with small duties around the house, but not without perpetual complaining, and Beauty still did the lion's share.

It grieved the father to see his children reduced to such circumstances, and he blamed himself severely. That first week Edmund would return from the fields with a cheerful whistle upon his lips, despite his blistered hands and sore muscles. But as the long days of labor continued, his shoulders began to droop with fatigue, and his whistle was less often heard. Beauty saw how her father took Edmund's weariness for sullenness, and how he read in it a silent accusation against himself. He also heard—with less imagination needed to interpret them into accusations—the vocal complaints of his two eldest daughters, and blamed himself all the more.

Seeing all this, Beauty was steeled with a new resolve to be cheerful herself, and make every effort to lift the spirits of her father and brother. She began a habit of singing or reading to them in the evenings, even when she was tired herself.

And so life fell into a sort of rhythm, and Beauty found joy in surprising places. For when you focus on another and their wants and comforts above your own, your own get all tied up with theirs. Watching her brother relish a dish that she had herself prepared, brought a warm glow to her heart. Seeing a smile flicker across her father's countenance brought a smile to her own.

Her sisters, however, continued wholly absorbed in their own misery, and so continued miserable.

The weather began to change; winter approached, but no snow had fallen.

Then one gusty evening, Mssr. Duveau came in with a letter.

When its contents were communicated, Estella and Mariette were sent into raptures, which they did not even attempt to contain. Oh, this was the end of their tribulation. They would soon be returning to their old life. The world would be made right again. They danced about the room and began planning their new wardrobes.

Beauty sat in silence, far less optimistic regarding the long term consequences of the letter.

As it happened, and as the letter communicated, one of Mssr. Duveau's ships had actually made it into harbor after having been thrown far off course by storms, and then becalmed for weeks on end, the crew nearly starving, and other various adventures which are much easier to read about than to live through. The letter also said that the majority of the cargo had made it safely into port.

Mssr. Duveau set out the very next day to claim his goods, for the dock-master who wrote the letter hinted that fees were accumulating with each passing day that the goods sat unclaimed in the dockyard's storehouse.

Estella and Mariette made up lists of things they wished their father to bring back for them. He took the lists, but said, "And if things do not go as well as we hope, what shall I bring you? If I can bring just one thing for each?"

Estella settled on a silken parasol. Mariette desired a pair of blue satin slippers. Their father looked to Beauty, who had made no list, and who now remained silent.

"What for you, Beauty? A new hat perhaps?" he asked.

"Nothing for me, papa, so long as you return home safely."

"Come, I would like to bring you something. Will you deny your father that joy?"

"I would like a rose, then. They do not grow here, and I miss them. I remember the hothouses at Market Street having them, even into the cold months."

The father smiled. "I shall bring you a whole bouquet of roses."

Mssr. Duveau arrived in Florens to find many complications and expenses awaiting him. A former creditor came forward and asserted rights to the majority of the goods. In order to defend his property, Duveau had to await the next assizes—nearly a month distant. He sent off a brief letter to his children, communicating that his stay in the city would be unavoidably prolonged, but without including any detail as to the cause. He spent a good deal of time gathering and arranging what papers and documents he could to substantiate his full rights of ownership, as well as to support his own claim that all debts toward the creditor had already been discharged. He sought out previous business partners who might stand witness for him, but this proved none too easy; most of his old acquaintance wanted nothing to do with him. Others, while feeling no ill-will toward him, were leery of standing in court.

Meanwhile, the dock-master began harboring a great dislike for Duveau, blaming him for upsetting the otherwise smooth flow of his dockyard. The long-nosed fellow urged Duveau continuously to have the goods removed from his storehouse as soon as may be, for the space was needed, and he did not hesitate to lay on Duveau all the fees and penalties he could. Duveau was forced, therefore, to find and rent a warehouse for the storage of goods he could not sell until after his rights to them were confirmed.

The snows of winter began to cover the city rooftops. The day of the assizes finally arrived. Alas, the prévôt was personal friends with Duveau's accuser and former creditor. They found means to invalidate at least part of Duveau's claims, and a portion of the goods were allotted to the corrupt moneylender—and likely some found its way into the pockets of his friend the prévôt.

By the time the goods remaining to him were finally sold, and all expenses were accounted for, Duveau had only a small fraction of the sum he had hoped to take away. It would be impossible to return his family to the city, even at a far lower standard of living than they had known previously. And he could not help but think it was better after all to stay away from the scenes of their old life. He had already experienced enough snubs and scorn from old acquaintances during his stay. He decided that he would use the little money that remained to better run the farm. There would be livestock to purchase in the spring, and a plow, and seed, and whatnot. He could hire more hands to help in the fields. Perhaps even another hired girl to help Beauty with the housework.

But he would bring back gifts for his children; on this he was determined. He found for Estella a beautiful silk parasol, and a lovely pair of satin slippers for Mariette. For Edmund's gift he decided on a flute of excellent craftsmanship. And for Beauty, a vase filled with pink roses.

Mssr. Duveau made it to Druane without incident. He rested there for a night at the inn. Early the next morning, when he wished to hire a cart to take him to Isole, they told him there was a storm coming in, and no one was willing to risk getting caught in it.

Then Duveau made a fateful decision. He decided to buy a horse and cart outright, and take his chances. The cart was by no means new, but in good repair. The horse was a large dapple-grey mare that he deemed would be suited to farm work. Duveau wasted no time haggling over the price. He paid what was asked and set out at once, gambling that he could outrun the storm. Moreover, he decided not to take the common road, but to cut straight through Inconnu Forest, reckoning that it was half the distance. He reasoned that even if the path was narrower and less smooth, it would still get him home in a shorter time. There were of course the tales of awful beasts and supernatural beings living in the Forest, but he did not believe such stories. He had his pistol if there were wolves.

There was no one to ask him, "Duveau, my dear chap, why would you risk the dangers of the Forest with a storm approaching? Were it not better to arrive home safely a day later, than never arrive home at all?"

If there had been anyone to ask such questions, Duveau would not have had a ready answer. The truth was, he did not think too deeply on the matter. He acted upon impulse, driven by an undefined desire to reach home as soon as possible. The rest of it he could not have explained. But any old gaffer who was native to those parts would have shaken his head knowingly and said that the Forest was luring him in.

At first the path was well marked, if a bit narrow, and he made good time. The sky was overcast, promising snow, but there was hardly a breath of wind. Duveau began to think the storm wouldn't come to much after all. At midday he stopped to rest and fodder the horse, and take a bite himself. When he started off again, it seemed like his afternoon would pass much as his morning had. And for an hour or two it did.

Then the snow began to fall, and the path became harder to distinguish. He went a little more slowly and cautiously. Uncertainty crept into his mind. Had he lost the path? No, no, there it was. Or was it? Surely that was it. Yes, it had to be.

An hour or so more, and the sky darkened as with nightfall, though it was not yet night. The snow fell more thickly. The wind became gusty and forceful; flurries of snowflakes obscured the trees. Shadows and shapes blended together. He reigned up his horse, and pulled his cloak more tightly around himself.

This would not do. He could scarce see the ground in front of his horse's feet; it was impossible to follow any sort of path—if indeed he was still on the path. He sat a moment considering what he had best do. Looking for shelter to wait out the storm seemed the only reasonable option. Perhaps if he could find a low-growing tree with dense branches...

Suddenly, a flash of lightning split the sky, followed closely by a low rumble of thunder, filling the air. The horse squealed and bolted.

The next few minutes were chaos: shapes looming up and blurring past, pounding hooves, jolting over uneven ground, snow in his eyes. Suddenly a tree loomed up right in front of him. The horse veered to narrowly miss it, but the cartwheel struck, and Duveau was thrown from his seat.

He landed in a snowbank and was dazed but unharmed. The horse had been arrested by the impact of the cart hitting the tree, and now stood trembling and heaving. The cart was tilted up on its side, the axle and one of the wheels broken and splintered.

Duveau got to his feet, and went to calm the horse. He stroked her head and spoke gently and reassuringly. Yet there was fear in his own heart. He disentangled her from the now useless harness and led her around to the tree-side of the upturned cart, where the tree and cart together provided some shelter against the wind. He tied her up and laid a blanket over her. There was nothing left to do but huddle down himself in the shelter of the cart and wait for the storm to pass.

He sat and tried not to let his mind wander to unpleasant things. Things like what he would do when the storm did pass, and he found himself in the midst of a trackless forest. After some time, he dozed and slept.

When he awoke, the wind had died down, and the snowflakes fell softly rather than being caught up in eddies. He guessed it to be the first watch of the night. He stood and stomped his feet to send the blood back into them. Then he checked that the horse was alright, and sat back down in his little nest of snow, with his back against the bottom of his cart.

He thought of his children, and he thought of his beloved wife. He wondered whether he would see her again if he died here in the snow.

Once more he dozed and slept.

Third Chapter

Duveau was startled from his sleep by a wolf's howl. The snow had ceased. There was a deep stillness. Perhaps the howl had been a dream. He looked up and saw the moon shining in the darkness above, with wisps of cloud moving across it.

Another howl sent a shiver down his spine, and proved that he had not dreamt the first. Then came another howl, and another. He realized that his one pistol would do very little against a pack of wolves, if they chose to attack. He trembled to think of them surrounding him, closing their circle gradually, and then rushing in to tear him limb from limb. The horse pranced uneasily, gave a distressed neigh, and started pulling against the rope that tied her. Duveau thought of mounting up and making a run for it, but the next moment, with a sudden jerk, the horse succeeded in breaking her bridle rope. Another moment and she had disappeared into the night. So it mattered not whether a desperate gallop would have been a wise course; it was no longer an option. He hoped the horse would make it safely away; he was sure he would never see her again.

The howls continued at irregular intervals, all around him. His situation seemed quite hopeless. He looked up at the moon, and decided he would not waste his last thoughts dwelling on his own demise. He thought of his beloved wife, and used her image to push the nasty images from his mind.

The next thing he knew, he was again awakening, though he did not recall falling asleep. The snowy forest was filled with a soft morning light. The storm was over and gone, but the ensuing calm filled him with a strange foreboding, rather than peace. The terrors of the night were past, but the day brought its own troubles.

By the light of morning, he could see the state of his cart, with his luggage and parcels tumbled out of it, some buried in snow, some broken. Beauty's vase must have fallen against another parcel, for it lay shattered in the snow, and her roses crushed.

He went through the mess, taking such items as he thought he could easily carry. He made a meager breakfast, trying to ration out what little provisions he had. Then he slung his makeshift sack over his shoulder and stood for a moment trying to reckon in which direction home lay.

When he did settle upon a direction, he was not entirely convinced it was the correct one. Yet he thought it was better to walk and possibly get somewhere than to sit and surely freeze. His progress was slow, for the snow was deep in places. He eventually came to a hill, stretching up before him, and decided to climb it. Perhaps the view from its summit could give him some clue as to his whereabouts.

He did make a discovery as he neared the crown, but it was not what he might have hoped. A wall of stone rose before him, at first only glimpsed through the trees, and then more visible as he neared it. His first impression was that it was a natural rock face. He could not discern its height. As near as he could guess, if he followed along the base of this crag, it would take him a little more west than he had planned, but still roughly in the direction he wished to go. And the snow was not deep here. So he decided to follow the rock, and see if it would give way.

He trudged on with the rock face on his right for almost an hour. He began to wonder how many leagues the wall extended. It seemed odd to him that such a prominent geographical boundary would not appear on any map—at least not any map he had ever seen.

Then he came to the gate, and stopped, arrested with awe as he gazed up at the great, imposing structure. Filling a narrow gap in the rock face, rising at least thirty feet high, was a gate somewhat resembling a wrought iron garden-gate, but on a giant scale. On a golden plaque, engraved in a clear, elegant script, were the following words:

Let he who desires enter

Curiosity and a hope for possible aid were equal factors in Duveau raising his hand to the gate. It swung inward with ease. He stepped through and shut the gate behind him. Then he fairly gasped, for here it was not snowy winter, as outside, but early spring. Bare branches were covered in tight buds, and the air was noticeably warmer. A wide path paved with bluish stones ran on before him, high groomed hedges on either side. As he walked along this avenue in a state of wonderment, the thought struck him that this must be the estate of some wealthy nobleman with recluse habits. An eccentric Duke perhaps.

Presently, he came out upon a green sward and caught his first view of the castle. It was an expansive stone structure with many towers and turrets, pillars and arches. There was no definite architectural style or era to which it belonged. At the far end of the sward, a little bridge carried him across a chattering stream, and he found himself on a garden path. Fountains and statues were interspersed amongst the shrubs and flowers and trees. The path here branched off, one way leading toward the castle, the other disappearing deeper into the gardens. He turned down the way which led toward the castle, and was soon mounting wide stone steps and passing under a great marble arch.

The door was as imposing as the gate had been, and appeared to be made of iron and oak. The knocker was a lion's head. He used it to make his presence known.

A few moments later, the door opened. Duveau stood hesitating, for no one appeared. After an awkward pause, he ventured inside. Still he saw no one. The hall in which he found himself had high painted ceilings and sculpted pillars. Light streamed in from tall windows.

The sound of the door closing startled him. He turned quickly toward it, but still could see no one. He walked with some trepidation to the far end of the hall, where a doorway opened onto a sitting room of some sort. A fire burned on the hearth there. He decided to sit and await the appearance of his host. Sitting in a comfortable chair and staring into the fire, he soon nodded off to sleep.

When he awoke, there was a tea tray on a table at his elbow. On it was toast and jam, scones and clotted cream, and a bowl of ripe fruit. Clearly it was meant for him. So after looking about the room and finding himself still alone, he took up a piece of toast and began spreading it with jam. A moment later he was wondering if it was really the best jam he'd ever tasted, or if he was just that hungry. When he turned his attention to his teacup, he found that it was already filled, and piping hot, as though it had just been poured a moment before. This struck him as very peculiar, but he tried not to let it bother him.

After taking his fill of tea and toast, scones and fruit, he walked over to the window to look out. It commanded a lovely view of the gardens. He decided to go out into them and explore a bit. He noticed when he passed the little table where he had enjoyed his tea, that the tea tray was gone and there was in fact no sign that it had ever been there. Without knowing exactly why, he quickened his step to leave the room.

Out in the gardens, he went down one path after another. He breathed in the delicate floral scents which filled the air, and felt thoroughly refreshed. He wondered how many gardeners it took to keep up such gardens. And then he recalled that he had not yet seen a single soul, and he could not shake the strange feeling that came over him. Surely there was some explanation; there was no such thing as magic, he told himself.

Then he came to a lovely stone arch covered in green vines and delicate blue flowers. It led into an enclosed garden, and a golden plaque stood prominently to one side of the archway. Upon the plaque were engraved the following words:

Let this garden be for the pleasure of all who enter;
Yet not one bud may be removed without consent.
He who disregards this,
His life is forfeit.

"How strange," Duveau said aloud to himself. He stepped through the vine-covered arch, and found himself in the most beautiful rose garden he had ever seen, with a fountain at the center of it. At first he thought the roses were white, but as he stepped forward a glint of green and yellow caught his eye. Then another glint of purple and blue. He stepped over and took a full bloom in his hand to examine it. The petals were iridescent, revealing a rainbow of varying colors as he turned the flower gently this way and that. It reminded him of the insides of sea-shells, and of opals. Beauty would be delighted with such a flower.

The words on the plaque came back to him. But surely that last bit was not to be taken literally. Such a kind person, whoever it was, that would open his house and grounds so hospitably—surely it was a hyperbole. And anyway, how could he ask permission when his host would not show himself? His presence was known; the tea tray convinced him of that. So why had he not been welcomed in person?

Then a new thought presented itself. What if the master of this estate was so far a recluse that he shunned all human interaction, even when it found him in his remote dwelling? What if the beauty of this place was merely a baited trap? What if the master of it was horribly disfigured? Or a madman? What if he really was the sort to kill a man if he was crossed?

Well, Duveau thought, *I'm not going to stay to find out.*

He had not found the help he had wished for—there had been no one to show him maps or give him directions to Isole—but at least when he left this place he would be no worse off than he had been.

He paused for a moment.

Who would know it if he did take a rose for Beauty? There was no one about. He was not in view of any castle windows. He would take just one and be on his way. He quickly plucked a rose and turned to leave the garden.

Then his heart stopped; his blood froze. There, beside the fountain, crouched an enormous beast.

He dropped the flower behind him, as though the beast had not seen what he had done. The creature had the shaggy black coat of a bear, the horns of a ram, the fangs and claws of a lion. Then Duveau heard a voice like a thunderous growl as the beast spoke.

"You have done the one thing I bid you not to do," the

creature said.

Duveau fell to his knees, overwhelmed by fear; it made his night with the wolves seem a trifling thing.

"But... sir," Duveau managed to say, "I would have asked you if you were here before. I trusted to your benevolence. I did not think it was so great a matter."

"Just because you did not see me, does not mean I was not here," the beast replied.

"That is hardly fair. How was I to know when I could not see you?"

"You should have asked."

"I was only thinking of my daughter. The flower was for her. I would never have picked it, but she asked for one especially."

The beast moved towards him.

"Please!" Duveau cried, trembling now with fear. "Don't kill me!"

"You still do not see," the beast said. "Your life is forfeit. That means you must stay here forever. But I will only have you on the condition that you stay willingly."

Duveau felt a glimmer of hope. "And if I am unwilling?"

"Then you must find someone who is willing to stay here in your stead."

"Then... then I may go? To look for such a person?"

"You may return to your children, if you will vow to bring another who is willing, or return yourself if such another is not to be found."

"Oh, thank you, sir," Duveau said, relief beginning to displace his fear.

"You shall leave in the morning, if that is your wish. Will you dine with me this evening?" the beast asked.

Duveau was somewhat startled by this request. It made him very uncomfortable, the idea of eating with such a creature. But he tried to hide his repulsion, terrified of giving offense.

"I... well... I'm very tired, you see... I do not wish to be rude, of course... if perhaps I could just..."

"Your dinner will be taken to you in your room, then," the beast said as he turned away. "Follow me."

Duveau was led back through the gardens, into the castle, then up a staircase, down a corridor, and into a large and richly furnished bedroom. It struck him how everything about the place now seemed so gloomy and ominous—quite different from the bright and welcoming appearance it had given upon his first arrival. Crossing the bedroom, the beast opened a door to reveal an adjoining dressing room. It looked more like the property room of a theater than an ordinary dressing room, for there were all manner of fancy and plain dress, for both sexes. There was everything from boots and shirts, to jewels and silks.

Then the beast did another unexpected thing. He indicated an empty trunk which sat open on the floor. "You may fill this trunk with anything here that you desire to take away with you."

When the beast had left him, Duveau could not help but feel relieved. He spent quite some time enjoyably looking through all of the finery, and choosing things for his children. The longer he looked, the more beautiful things he found, so that many times he had to take out again what he had put into the trunk, to make room for the new items. At length, he found a little chest of solid gold filled with costly gems. After adding this, he was at last satisfied with the trunk's contents, and shut the lid.

He went back into the bedroom and found a little table had been set up with enough food to feed half a dozen men. There was roast beef with savory sauce, baked vegetables with spices, warm bread with butter, and broiled fish with lemon. The wine was excellent, but he could find no vintage on the bottle.

He lay awake most of that night, thinking over his life, and trying to make sense of recent events. He could not reconcile the actions of the beast, one moment so horribly cruel, and the next so generous and obliging.

It seemed incongruous. Surely the seeming kindness was only a front, to hide malicious intent. The whole estate was deceitfully beautiful to veil the ugliness of its master, he thought.

He realized he was only going home to say farewell to his children. For no one would willingly come to this place unless tricked, and no one would willingly stay once they'd learned the truth. He would have to return himself. He was thoroughly convinced that if he did not fulfill his promise, there would be death to pay. No matter if he were to go to the ends of the earth, the creature would find him. Whether he would be hunted, and die in agony by tooth and claw, or whether the monster could reach him some other way, he did not know. Perhaps his heart would simply stop. There was some sorcery about it all.

Fourth Chapter

The morning came at last. The remains of his dinner had been cleared away, and a breakfast was laid. Presently there was a knock. It was the beast to show him down to the door. Duveau hesitated, turning toward the dressing room.

The beast read his thought. "My servants have already taken down the trunk."

Before the door of the castle was drawn up a carriage worthy of any nobleman, with two fine white horses in the harness. The beast turned to Duveau, and in his growling voice asked, "Do you vow to return, or else send one willing to take your place?"

"I do," Duveau said soberly. He was strangely reminded of his wedding vows, with a weighty feeling of irrevocable commitment.

Once more the beast did an unexpected thing. "This is for your daughter."

He handed Duveau one of the iridescent roses. Duveau did not know what to say, so he bowed his thanks, and climbed into the carriage. The horses set off immediately, and he was born away at great speed. Before he knew it, he was passing through snowy woods.

Early in the afternoon he found himself entering the familiar regions surrounding his farm. These were certainly not ordinary horses, he thought. They went on at such a marvelous rate and did not seem to tire.

When Estella and Mariette saw their father driving up in a splendid carriage, they ran out to meet him, full of excitement.

"Why father," Mariette called before he had fairly lighted. "You had us all worried. Your letter made it seem as though nothing would be changed."

Edmund and Beauty came out also to greet their father. It was Edmund who noticed that no one was driving the horses. "Why, where is the coachman?"

His father ignored the question and said, "I have gifts for you all."

The trunk could not be lifted, but its contents were unloaded. Estella and Mariette were soon squealing and giggling over all the finery.

"And for you, Beauty," her father said, giving her the rose. "Little might you guess how much it has cost me."

Beauty was alarmed. She recognized the look on her father's face; she had seen it once before, when he had told her that her mother was gone forever. She felt intuitively that a matter of life and death was about to be disclosed. "Oh papa, what is it?"

Then the whole story came out. He told them all his adventures, and their consequences.

Edmund was of the opinion that the horrible beast-creature would not really come after him, and so he need not go back, but live happily forgetting the creature's existence. Estella and Mariette quickly agreed to this view.

Their father insisted that he must keep his promise. Indeed, he was quite petrified to break the vow he had made.

Beauty had stood silently all the while, a strange battle going on inside her. She did love her father; she would have liked to think she loved him enough to take his place. But she also feared the unknown creature. Then again, the wondrous beauty of the castle and its gardens drew her, even though her father described them as an evil façade. There was some mystery about the place, and its master; something deep inside her longed to uncover that mystery. But her father said the beast and his castle were full of trickery and deceit. It was not safe. Yes, but the strange longing would not go away, despite the opposition of her fear.

Suddenly she spoke. "I will go."

"What?" Everyone turned to look at her.

Beauty went on in a calm, steady voice. "He said one willing could take your place."

"He did say that," Duveau said, taking his daughters hands, "but I would rather go myself than let you take my place."

"If we go and kill the horrid beast, then no one will have to stay with him," Edmund said.

"Do not speak so!" his father implored, casting a nervous glance at the carriage and horses, as though fearful that they would bring back tales to their master. "There is some powerful sorcery or magic about him. I doubt he could be killed by ordinary means."

"I will go," Beauty said again.

"No, Beauty," her father insisted, "I cannot let you."

"I suppose the carriage is waiting to take someone back," Edmund said.

"Yes." The father did not trust his voice to say more. He climbed into the carriage, feeling like it was the last thing in the world he wanted to do. He said goodbye to his children, and waited to be carried away. But the carriage did not move.

"I am ready," he said aloud. Several awkward minutes passed. He repeated his goodbyes, and again waited, but still the horses did not start. At last he climbed out of the carriage.

"I don't understand it," he said.

"I think..." Beauty paused. "He said you must go willingly. Perhaps you go only because you feel you have no choice. Papa, I am willing."

Her father was not convinced. "More likely the creature means to allow me one last night of freedom, and I may start back tomorrow."

"Goodbye Ed," Beauty said tenderly, embracing her brother.

He almost pushed her away. "Don't be daft, Beauty. You're not going anywhere."

Beauty was undeterred. "Goodbye Stella. Goodbye Mary. Goodbye papa." She embraced them each in turn.

Her father did not think much of her theory. "They

won't budge for you any more than they did for me. It is as I said. He means me to start off in the morning."

Beauty stepped into the carriage before anyone could stop her. No sooner was the carriage door shut, than the horses set off at a brisk canter. She waved her hand out of the window, but her family was soon out of sight.

Her thoughts sped along as quickly as the horses. There were still many items left on her day's list of chores. She went through each task in her mind. Who would do them now? The bread was still in the oven for supper; she hoped Annie, the hired girl, would remember to take it out before it burned. She pictured how melancholy the meal would be, when their father's return ought to have been joyous.

Who would make sure father's slippers were warmed by the fire? And who would read to them in the evenings? How would they manage without her? The tears came, blurring her vision. Watching the trees speed past started to make her dizzy, so she turned her attention to the inside of the carriage.

Embroidered curtains of blue and white were tied back with silken cords. The seats had cushions of dark blue velvet. Her eye fell upon the rose that lay in her lap; she had forgotten she was holding it. It sent her thoughts forward, instead of dwelling on what was behind. She wondered what it was like, this place she was going to— the place where she must spend her forever. Would she be locked up in a tower? Would there be anyone to talk to? She began to feel frightened.

As the last light of day faded, she made a discovery which caused her to temporarily forget her fear: the petals of the rose she held glowed with a faint light of their own. She could see the flashes of iridescence even in the darkness. Never had she seen anything so wonderfully beautiful.

Long before she had expected to arrive, she found the carriage was slowing to a stop. The horses drew up in front of wide stone steps, presumably leading up to an entrance. She could not see much of the castle in the dark, but there were great torches lighting the steps, and she could see lights away in the garden.

The carriage door was opened for her, though she saw no one. As she stepped down she was aware that a great creature stood at the top of the steps. It must be the beast. She was afraid to look at him, her father's description coming to the forefront of her mind.

"Welcome." The voice was not what she had expected.

She dared to raise her eyes to the top of the steps. There was no doubt the creature was hideous. His fangs were visible even when his mouth was shut. She shuddered to think of inciting his wrath. She quickly lowered her eyes again. "I have come in my father's stead, to be your prisoner."

"Not a prisoner," the beast replied. "Come."

She followed him into the castle, though none too closely. He led her through one passage after another, now down a few steps, then up a few more, until they came to a beautiful door of carved wood. He opened it for her, and then stood to one side.

"These will be your chambers," he said. "If you are in want of anything, you have but to ask. Your breakfasts will be served to you here. The days you may spend as you please; the castle and its grounds are yours to explore and enjoy. I ask only that you dine with me in the evenings."

Beauty was not a little surprised. She could go about the castle as she pleased? And the gardens as well? This seemed quite a magnanimous gesture. But then, her father had said the creature was unpredictably generous. She was sure his cruel side would come out soon enough.

"Yes, certainly," she said. It would be no good

angering him right at the beginning by refusing to dine with him.

"It is very late, so this once your dinner will be taken up to you, but I will see you tomorrow evening. Now I bid you goodnight."

"Goodnight," Beauty replied.

When she was safely alone in her room, she stood for a moment with her back against the door, taking in her surroundings. A fire burned brightly on the hearth. There was a well-filled bookcase of dark wood set into one wall. A few tapestries covered some of the other walls. To one side of the fire, near enough to benefit by its light but not so near as to scorch one's face, stood a large wing-back chair. A small round table was placed beside the chair, with a slender vase of painted porcelain in the center of it. Could it have been put there especially for her rose? She went over to the table and found the vase was indeed prepared with water, so she placed her rose inside. Perhaps it was her imagination, or the uncertain firelight, but it seemed the petals perked up as soon as the stem touched the water. She stood a moment admiring the firelight playing upon the petals.

Presently, a delicious smell drew her attention. A chair was drawn up invitingly to a table near the center of the room. The table was laden with more dishes than she could name, and lighted by numerous candles. The sight and smell reminded her of her hunger, and she sat herself down to eat. She thought she would try tasting every dish, but as she worked her way through, she found several of them to be so delicious that she was inclined to take a larger helping. Before long, she was quite full, and there were still dishes untasted. She acknowledged herself defeated, and pushed back her chair with a contented sigh.

She cast a glance around the room. "I'm so tired," she thought aloud.

No sooner had she spoken than her eye fell upon the door leading into her bedroom; it stood open and she could see that candles were already burning there. When she entered, she found the coverlet was turned back, and a nightgown had been laid out. The bed looked very comfortable. She undressed, slipped into the nightgown, and climbed between the sheets. The moment after her head touched the pillow, she was asleep.

Fifth Chapter

When Beauty awoke in the morning, a pretty little gilt clock on the wall across from her bed was chiming a pleasant tune. The hour was eleven; she had not slept so late in a very long time. She lay for several minutes trying to remember her dream, but could not. It had been such a lovely dream. If only she could remember it.

The remains of her dinner had vanished, and the table was now spread with bread and butter, hot porridge and cream, little cakes of various kinds, and jam and honey for good measure. The cakes had a rather wholesome flavor, not being very sweet. Beauty liked them best spread with honey.

When she had finished her breakfast, she decided to explore her rooms a bit. Her first discovery was a large glass door opening off of her bedroom, obscured by a thick green curtain. It opened onto a little portico covered in vines; the light that came through was made soft and cool by the canopy of leaves. The far end of the portico led into a perfect tunnel of greenery, and at the end of the tunnel, she could see the bright light of midday shining on purple and yellow flowers, and a path which quickly disappeared out of her view. She thought she had better dress before going out to explore the path.

Her next discovery was the wardrobe. She was amazed and delighted by its array of dresses. There were simple frocks, and elegant ball gowns, and everything in between. And every dress she tried on fit her perfectly. It is not to be wondered at that she got a little carried away, and took two hours to choose which dress she would wear for her garden excursion. At last, she settled on a lavender colored frock with a soft layered skirt.

As she traversed the green tunnel, she was met with a delicate earthy smell. She closed her eyes and took a deep breath; a smile lit her countenance. That was only the beginning. Every path she went down greeted her with a new and delightful scent. Some flowers she recognized, others she had never seen before. The colors and shapes were wonderful, the contrasts often unexpected. One flower she found particularly fascinating. It was not bold and striking like some of the others. It had a rather ordinary looking bud with a funny texture and a drab sort of coloring, but the blooms opened like oyster-shells, revealing a glistening interior of creamy white. A small sphere like a pearl was nestled inside. Maybe it was a pearl, but she was too afraid to touch it.

At every turn there was another tree, or topiary, or statue, or fountain. Whenever she thought she had discovered the most beautiful part of the gardens, she would round a corner and find beauty to rival or surpass it.

She was surprised to notice the daylight beginning to fade; the whole afternoon had passed her by. She wondered that she had not found the enclosed garden where her father had plucked the forbidden rose.

Well, I only have forever, Beauty thought. *I'm sure to find it sooner or later.*

She had no trouble finding her way back to her rooms. Tea was waiting for her in the room where breakfast had been. A fire burned in the fireplace, as well as enough candles to cast light into every corner. After refreshing herself with tea and fruit, she went to peruse the bookshelves. She found several books that interested her, chose one, and sat down to read until dinner time.

Half an hour passed, and Beauty began to worry about the approaching meal. She found herself rereading the same sentences over and over. At last she set the book aside. Should she dress for dinner? Perhaps it would not be expected. She somehow doubted that the rules and forms of "nice society" were observed in this castle. Then again, she certainly did not wish to offend or anger the beast by making an erroneous assumption. She went into her bedroom undecided, and there found her answer: a lovely evening gown had been laid out for her. That certainly meant that she was supposed to dress for dinner. She wished that she had a lady's maid to help her, but set about to manage as best she could.

And then an odd thing happened, for as she began to put on the dress, it was almost as though the dress itself was assisting her. No, that wasn't it. It was rather as though an invisible lady's maid were in fact helping her to dress. That's when the notion of invisible servants first entered Beauty's head. It was a little unnerving, so she tried not to think about it anymore. When she had finished dressing, she went back into her sitting room to wait, unsure what to expect.

Before long, there was a knock on her door.

"Enter," Beauty called as she rose from her seat. The door opened, and a floating candelabra appeared. The idea of invisible servants seemed to be substantiated, for the candelabra floated at just the height it might be if a tall man were holding it. It's movements likewise corroborated the idea that it was carried by an invisible hand. Beauty followed the candelabra without a word, as it led her through various passages and anterooms, until they reached a great hall.

The floor was of green and white marble. An enormous chandelier accented with gold and crystal hung from the ceiling. Carved marble pillars were inlaid with turquoise and onyx. Curtains of fine linen, blue and green in color, were draped and tied with white cords. The walls, where visible, were carved with images, and along the top portion, adorned with gold. The hearth was the size of a small room, and a roaring fire cast a warm glow.

There, at the far end of the room, standing beside the chair at the head of the table, was the beast. Beauty approached him with her eyes downcast, afraid that if she looked at his awful figure, she would lack the fortitude to draw near. The beast greeted her calmly, and she took the seat prepared for her.

She found herself to be quite nervous. The first course

began in silence, which Beauty was unsure how to break, but felt that she ought, so as not to give offense. She occupied herself with her plate, and racked her brain, but to no avail. The beast suddenly spoke, asking if Beauty had enjoyed her day.

"Yes," she replied.

"What did you do?"

Beauty thought that perhaps the beast would be gratified if she were to show how impressed she was with the gardens, and so went into a rather detailed account of her afternoon, describing her joy, or wonder, at each memorable thing she had encountered. The beast interjected here and there, mostly to ask or answer a question. She learned that pearls could indeed be harvested from the oyster-flowers.

In the middle of the fourth course, Beauty happened to glance over at the beast, and immediately regretted it. His fangs and claws were most disturbing. She quickly looked down at her own plate, and waited in silence for the next course. After a time, the beast attempted to reawaken the conversation. But Beauty could not get the image of those cruel fangs out of her mind's eye, and her replies were brief.

By the end of the fifth course she began wondering how many courses there could be. The sixth course was eaten in total silence, and Beauty didn't know whether to be grateful or alarmed. At last the seventh and final course was finished, and the beast rose. Beauty followed his example.

Then the beast did a shocking thing. He stood before her and asked a simple question: "Beauty, will you be my wife?"

Beauty was terrified. She was overwhelmed by the thought that if she refused, he would eat her right there; her life would end in agony. Or worse, she would be punished but not killed, living on in continual pain, until she was driven mad and wished for death.

"Oh, what shall I say?" she asked herself, not realizing in her distress that she had spoken aloud.

"You shall say honestly 'yes', or 'no', without fear," the beast said.

"No," Beauty replied quickly.

"Then I bid you goodnight," was all the beast said.

Beauty turned and followed the floating candelabra back to her rooms. She wondered at the beast's question, and that he had shown no anger at her refusal. She was helped out of her dress by invisible hands, and went to bed.

When she awoke the next morning, the little gilt clock was chiming its pleasant tune. She had had another wonderful dream, and this time she could remember something of it. There had been a prince. And he had given her a rose, just like the iridescent one her father had given her from the beast's garden. She couldn't remember anything else, except that the prince had been noble and kind. She could not recall his face, but had the distinct impression that he had been charming and handsome.

That day she decided to spend in exploring the interior of the castle. This required some courage, for she was terrified by the thought of opening some door or other and happening upon the beast. It was his castle after all. She wondered if he would treat her differently after her refusal of the night before. But such thoughts she pushed away. She already had to spend hours in his company at dinner; why should she torment herself with the thought of him at other times?

She went down the passage from her door, walking slowly as there were many tapestries and other curiosities to admire. She soon came to a crossing of ways, where another passage joined hers, and decided to go left. This passage was lined with suits of armor, polished to perfection. Presently she came to an enormous spiraling staircase. It had a dark wooden railing, carved intricately all the way up. At the top was a sort of landing with a tall window of colored glass to her left, a door to her right, and a large open archway straight before her.

She passed under the archway, and found herself in a long gallery, all windows on the left. The floor was covered in black and green carpeting. The high ceiling was covered in frescoes of amazingly rich and varied colors, depicting sundry scenes of people and places. Beauty thought they might be historical scenes, and she gazed up at them for quite some time trying to see if she could identify any of them. But if they were historical, it was not any history with which she was familiar. As she looked, she saw many creatures not quite human, which she had not noticed at first, playing prominent roles. If Beauty had not in fact spoken with a beast only the night before, she would have immediately drawn the conclusion that the paintings were inspired by myth and legend. As it was, she thought it no less likely that they were historical.

Her neck began to ache with the strain of looking up at the ceiling so long, and she turned her attention to the wall on her right. It was lit to full advantage by the windows opposite, and was covered in frames of widely differing sizes. Some were heavy, prominent frames, others were thin, elegant frames, and each contained a painting. One in particular caught her eye. She walked over to it, to inspect it more closely.

At first she couldn't tell what the painting was of, for the colors seemed to be only smudges, blurring together. But the longer she looked, the more clear the picture became. It was a knight mounted on a black charger, riding through trees, with a castle in the distance. And still, the longer she looked, the more detail she saw. There were wildflowers growing in patches along the knight's path, and birds in the trees, and a banner waving from a tower of the castle.

Beauty stood engrossed. Soon she saw the very leaves of the trees, and the links of the knight's armor. It grew more and yet more clear, until it became life-like, and then went on to become somehow more than life-like. As with eagle eyes, she saw the face of a lady looking out from one of the castle windows, and could distinguish her features as though the lady were standing in the room beside her.

Beauty was marveling at the individual hairs of the horse's tail, when she started suddenly. Had the tail moved? Yes, the horse was swishing its tail! The entire picture came alive, as though she were watching the scene from a window herself. She watched the progress of the knight, and when he reached the castle, he seemed to be talking to the lady, wooing her perhaps. The lady seemed reluctant. Beauty felt there was some secret that the lady feared the knight would discover.

And then Beauty was startled again, and almost took a step back. The beams of a setting sun shone on the lady's face and she was no longer a beautiful lady, but a deformed hag, so ugly it made Beauty uncomfortable to look upon her. But she watched with deep interest the knight's response.

He threw off all cumbersome parts of his armor, climbed the wall of the castle with the help of some vines, and entered the lady-hag's window. She was kneeling with her face buried in her hands, apparently crying bitterly. The knight, ever so tenderly, drew her hands from her face and seemed to speak lovingly to her. She resisted, but he was gently persistent. From the look in his eyes, which Beauty could somehow see quite plainly, the knight seemed to see something different than Beauty saw when looking at the hag. The knight bent and kissed the lady-hag's brow, and the scene suddenly froze. It was only a painting again, but now of a castle surrounded by trees with a knight kissing an ugly, deformed woman at one of the windows.

Beauty blinked, with a feeling as of waking from some strange dream. But shouldn't the kiss have broken the spell? Why was the lady still an ugly hag? Beauty didn't like it. She turned to another painting. This one was much like the other in that it started out as indistinct smudges and grew more and more clear the longer she looked at it. She stood for quite some time, always seeing more detail in the painting, but this one did not come alive.

At last she turned to a third painting, and had a similar experience. This third painting she liked best. It was of a beautiful green valley, a shining lake, and snowy mountains in the distance. There was a fishing boat on the lake, and a pair of fishermen that seemed in the very act of drawing up their nets with their day's catch. But this picture did not come alive either.

Beauty then decided to continue exploring other rooms, but would be sure to return to the picture gallery another time. It would certainly take several afternoons to look at all the pictures that hung there. She went back under the archway, and tried the door near the top of the stairs.

She found herself in an oblong room, with the sunlight filtering in through a glass portion of the roof. At the far end, which was one of the narrower walls, there stood a great grandfather clock, ticking away loudly. The long wall on the left was covered with tapestries, interrupted by a single door. The wall to the right likewise, although its door was nearer the grandfather clock than the other.

She tried first the door nearest her, and found behind it an enormous room filled with sculptures. Some were of maidens and warriors, others of mothers and fathers and children. Some showed workmen at their craft, and others workmen at rest. In fact, there were all sorts of people doing all sorts of things. There were animals also; small animals, and large animals, all life-like in their proportions. There were many mythical-looking creatures that she was not familiar with, and she wondered if any such really existed. After an incomplete survey, again making a mental note to return at some future time, she went back into the glass-roofed passage and tried the second door.

This room was even larger than the first, and filled with wood-carvings of every description. There were elegant and intricate patterns, and puzzles, and carvings within carvings. There were quite a few pieces which seemed to defy both logic and the laws of nature, and Beauty wondered how they could have been made. Thus she meandered through the carvings, now stopping, now moving on, all the while marveling at the exquisite and inscrutable workmanship. The inkling of a desire was born in her bosom, to be able to carve and craft such beauty with her own hands.

There were also seven pillars supporting a ceiling so high, Beauty almost felt that she was out of doors. Each pillar was carved out of living wood, out of which grew green vines and blossoms, each pillar having a different colored blossom. She wondered how they could grow without sunlight. It was then she realized that though the room was filled with a warm, golden light by which everything was illuminated, she could not discover from whence it came. There did not seem to be any windows, nor candles, nor torches. Yet the very air seemed suffused with light. It remained an unsolved mystery.

When she at last returned again to the oblong passage, the grandfather clock told her tea would be waiting in her room, so she retraced her steps down the spiraling staircase, past the suits of armor, and finally through the passage off of which her own rooms opened. As she expected, she found tea spread, with cakes and fruit piled on elegant silver platters. She wondered how the servants—if there really were invisible servants—

always timed everything so perfectly to accommodate her; all the tea things were hot and fresh, as though just laid out a moment before.

After taking some refreshment from the well-laden tea table, she curled up to finish the book she had begun the day before. It was about two sisters, one lazy and querulous, the other sweet and industrious. Beauty could not help but think of her own sisters and herself as she read. And the more she read, the more she identified with the diligent sister. She was even the youngest, as Beauty was. And she always desired to make those around her happy, as Beauty did. But eventually the story took an unexpected turn. The elder daughter was met by a wizard, who tested her, as masters of the magical arts often do in storybooks. Predictably, she refused to do the task he asked of her, and complained that it was unreasonable of the wizard to even suggest it. Then the wizard showed the girl her own heart, and it was black and ugly indeed. (Here Beauty thought the story was going just as she expected.) But the girl was stricken with grief and remorse when she saw thus plainly her own ugliness, and she went away in tears.

Then the younger sister met the same wizard, who likewise tested her. She very cheerfully agreed to do as he asked. When she had completed the task, she went to tell him it was done. Then, just as he had done for her sister, the wizard showed the girl her own heart, and it was black and ugly indeed. (Here Beauty exclaimed aloud her disapproval of this ridiculous story.) The girl told the wizard that he was a wicked man, and a deceitful one, for she knew herself to be good. And she went away feeling self-satisfied and unjustly treated. She never saw the wizard again, and went on living as she had.

The last paragraph of the story told of the elder sister, who sought out the wizard. She soon found him, and begged him with the tears flowing from her eyes if there was any way to make her heart beautiful, and if so, that he would show her what she must do.

That was the end. Beauty stared for a moment at the last page, as though expecting a more satisfying ending to appear. Then she shut the book with an exasperated sigh, and almost threw it down on the table. Why was everything in this castle so vexing? The paintings didn't tell nice stories, and the books didn't tell nice stories. It was all very annoying.

Just then, the knock sounded which meant she was to be escorted by a floating candelabra to dinner. At the moment, she found this too annoying. As she traversed the passages toward the great hall, with the suspended light moving on before her, she determined not to look at the beast at all, if she could help it, remembering how it had affected her before. Once again she wondered if he would be angry with her for refusing to be his wife. Perhaps he would not speak to her; they could eat in silence and she could pretend she was alone.

She entered the great hall, and approached the table. The beast greeted her, and she replied politely, ever fearful of inciting his wrath. Attempting to hide the vexation that still occupied her mind, Beauty took her seat, careful not to look at the beast. Even his shadow was frightful. She was somewhat mortified to realize just then that she had not dressed for dinner; she was still wearing the simple gown she had worn all day. But the beast did not seem to take notice—at least, he said nothing about it. The first course was brought, and begun in silence. And then the beast asked suddenly, as he had done the day before, how she had spent her day.

"I found the picture gallery, and I read a book," she said, hoping he would be satisfied with this answer. For a time it seemed he would be; the rest of that course was finished in silence. But as they started into the second course, the beast spoke again.

"What was the book?"

Beauty gave the title.

"You did not like it?"

"No," Beauty said. "Have you read it?"

"I know it, yes. It is two separate stories, really; one is very sad, and one is full of hope."

Beauty left the conversation once more to die. She did not wish to share her inmost thoughts with a beast. And yet, she did wish there was someone with whom she could share them. The prince from her dream suddenly came to her mind. She thought what a pity it was that he was only a dream.

The second course was finished and the third begun. Then once more the beast spoke.

"Stories are not always written to be liked."

"What?" Beauty had been lost in her own thoughts. Hers was the quick reply of one who has been caught not paying attention. A moment later her bewilderment faded as her brain started processing and analyzing what the beast had said. "Do you mean that the author intended the story to be disliked? It rather makes one feel tricked into reading it."

"A story may be written with a purpose other than simply entertaining the reader."

"You are suggesting that the story I read today had such a purpose?"

"I am."

Perhaps it had something to do with her momentary

befuddlement when she had been startled out of her own thoughts, or perhaps it was something in the beast's tone and manner, but somehow Beauty had unconsciously been drawn into a conversation she had determined beforehand not to enter. "Well, what was its purpose then?"

The beast answered with another question. "What part did you dislike?"

"The ending. It was a terrible ending."

"Perhaps because it was really a beginning," the beast said. "Many of the best books end with a beginning."

"And I didn't like the wizard character. Why did he show the truth to one sister and trick the other?"

"Did he?"

"Well of course he did. The younger sister didn't have a black heart, but he showed her a black heart as though it were hers."

"How do you know it was not her heart?"

"Because she was good."

"Was she? Hearts cannot be judged by exteriors."

Beauty did not acknowledge it to herself in the moment, but her defense of the younger sister was piqued by her feeling a kinship with the character. "She did as he asked cheerfully; she passed his test."

"Perhaps that wasn't the test after all."

Beauty fell silent, but her eyes, fixed on her plate, betrayed that her thoughts were not idle. She did not speak again until the fourth course was concluded.

"Do you mean that seeing their own heart was the test?" she asked suddenly.

"And if it was?" the beast prompted.

"Then her fault was in her response. She was unwilling to accept the possibility that she wasn't what she thought herself to be. It was pride then that blackened her heart."

If Beauty had looked, she would have seen the beast smile before he spoke. "Pride is one of those vices that can hide quite comfortably behind an appearance of goodness. The motives of the heart are not easily judged."

Beauty did not venture a reply.

"Do you still dislike the story?" the beast asked.

"I'm not sure," was Beauty's answer; she was still bothered by it.

By this time they were enjoying the fifth course. The dishes had all been so rich, however, that Beauty was quite full, and rather dreading two more courses. But presently the beast rose, indicating that the fifth course was to be the last. Beauty rose likewise, much relieved.

She was quite startled when the beast stood before her and asked, "Beauty, will you be my wife?"

Hadn't she already given her answer? "No," she said, in some confusion.

"Then I bid you goodnight."

Beauty returned to her rooms, puzzling over the evening as a whole, and particularly its conclusion. As she could make nothing of it, she put it from her mind, and went to bed.

Sixth Chapter

In the morning Beauty awoke knowing she had dreamt again of her prince, but unable to remember any particulars of the dream. There were only the words echoing in her mind, the tone a mixture of urgent warning and ardent plea: "Do not trust appearances."

Was it her prince who had said it? She thought probably it was, but since she couldn't remember the dream, she had no idea of the context.

In her exploratory wanderings that afternoon, she happened upon the aviary. For over an hour she had walked through the castle, so that she began to marvel at its vastness. Through many beautiful rooms she walked, of various sizes and descriptions. Up many a staircase she ascended, and down many another. She passed through doors and under arches, some of wood, some of masonry, some plain, some carved or sculpted.

At length, she opened an arched door, like many another she had already passed through, and suddenly found herself outdoors—except not quite outdoors. It was something like a courtyard, enclosed on all sides by a quadrangle of the castle, yet unlike a courtyard, for a domed roof of crystalline glass, reinforced with iron muntins, enclosed it above. Beauty thought that she would very much like to sit here on a rainy day, and watch the rain play upon the domed glass.

The greenery which filled the quadrangle was of kinds unfamiliar to her. The air was cool and sweet. The myriad songs of innumerable birds filled the place. And there was no discord, though the voices and tones were so varied. The birds were so tame and fearless that Beauty's presence did not disturb them in the least.

There was one small red bird with grey-tipped wings that seemed to take an especial liking to her. For some time it hopped along the path behind her as she meandered through the enclosure. Then it flew up to land on a branch near her head and chirped at her.

She paused for a moment to smile at it, and then walked past. But the little bird only flew to another branch in front of her, tenaciously seeking her attention. And when, a moment later, Beauty turned to admire a lovely blue and white bird that had landed nearby, the little red bird twittered loudly and hopped on its branch in protest.

Beauty began to find Little Red to be a nuisance. She did not owe the bird her attention, and the persistence with which her attention was demanded was not putting her in a mood to give it. Somehow the creature reminded her of Mariette.

At length, the little bird made its boldest move yet, and flew up to land on her forearm. It then side-stepped along in a rather comical fashion, till it sat in her hand. She stroked its head and back, and even then it would not be quiet, but cooed and twittered, though now in a more contented strain.

"Stupid little bird," Beauty muttered aloud.

She had a very strong desire to silence the creature. Then the thought came suddenly that it would be quite easy to crush it, as it rested, so small and fragile, in her hand. A strange feeling of power over the creature possessed her, and an unaccountable curiosity. Could she do it? Would she do it? The stupid little thing looked up at her with innocent and trusting eyes, and yet, she found the feeling of power only increase at the utter helplessness of the creature in her hands.

All of this happened in a single moment. The next, she was overwhelmed with horror at her own thoughts and set the bird down hastily, fearing what she might do. Why would she think such a thing? She didn't want the bird to die; that was not like her at all. She would never harm an innocent creature; she was not the sort of person to take a life. She shuddered. Perhaps it was some influence of the castle working upon her—corrupting her.

There she stopped herself, as she was reminded of the story she had read only the day before. How could she be sure it was not her own wicked impulse? Did she know herself to be good? Could she know such a thing? She did not want to be blinded by pride, unwilling to be wrong and unreceptive to correction.

She decided she had had enough of the aviary for one day. Eager to distract herself from the unpleasant thoughts that filled her head, she found her way back to her rooms, selected a volume from the bookcase, and lost herself within its pages till dinnertime.

That evening, as she sat at dinner with the beast's form looming beside her, she could not keep herself from wondering if he had ever killed anyone. She considered asking him, her curiosity striving against her fear. She wanted to know, though she was afraid of what the answer might be.

Dinner progressed; there was some polite conversation. The aviary was mentioned, and Beauty learned that it was home to forty-nine different kinds of birds. All the while, one recurring question was in her thoughts. Many times she made up her mind to ask it, opened her lips to speak, and then changed her mind again. There were a few more attempts at conversation, interrupted by long intervals of silence.

At last, Beauty set down her spoon after finishing a pudding, and suddenly blurted out, "Have you ever taken a life?"

"I have." There was no hesitation in the calm reply.

Beauty was as much offended as alarmed by this blunt and seemingly callous response. She checked her rising emotions, and asked, "Intentionally?"

"Yes."

Beauty wished herself a thousand leagues away; she wished never to see or speak to the beast again. He was a killer, and he was not even ashamed of it. He was an unfeeling brute. She remembered the strange feeling of power when the little bird lay helplessly in her hand, and attributed the same to the beast. She had never seen him in a rage, and wondered if he was prone to fits of temper. Then she pictured him standing over his helpless victim, dispassionate and indifferent, killing on a whim, and that seemed more terrifying even than an act of violent passion.

When they stood from the table, she had to stifle an impulse to run from the room. In her general indignation, she was not even surprised when the beast asked, "Beauty, will you be my wife?"

There was both anger and reckless defiance in her voice when she replied, "No, I will not."

She half expected a violent retaliation to her insolence, but the beast replied in gentle tones, "Then I bid you goodnight."

When once more in her own bedroom, she threw herself on the bed without undressing, and lay there unsure whether she wanted most to scream or cry. He was a despicable creature. He may show her kindness, but it was all deceit; she knew his heart was cruel. She hated him for his duplicity. She may not have realized it, but she hated him for not being as she wished him to be. She thought of her prince, and his warning to not trust appearances. How true his words had proved. She lay there smoldering for quite some time, wishing to think of anything except the beast, and thinking of nothing but the beast. Eventually, she fell asleep.

Even in her dream she was distressed, but her prince was there to comfort her. He did not say a word, only held her tenderly in his arms. She cried bitterly upon his chest, until her tears were spent. Then a sweet solace came over her, and she woke. She lay for a time, reluctant to rise, as the dream faded away, and only the inexpressible feeling of peace remained.

Her clock suddenly chimed in its dulcet tones, telling her the hour was ten. When she opened her eyes and sat up, the sweet contented feeling suddenly dissipated. Her prince was only a dream-prince after all. A strong feeling of loneliness overcame her like a wave of the sea, and she was dragged into melancholy by the undertow. She had no appetite for breakfast.

She fell back on her pillows and stared at the ceiling for some time. Then she roused herself and got up, only to sit in a chair and stare out of the window. She did not feel like reading. She did not even feel like thinking.

She missed Edmund. The sun began to descend the western sky. Suddenly she got up; she would go to the picture gallery.

Upon entering the gallery, her attention was immediately drawn to a door at the far end of it, which she had not noticed before. Behind it was a dimly lit room, much smaller than the gallery. There were no windows she could discern, but a thick curtain covered the far wall. She went to it and pulled the braided golden cord which hung at one side. Up went the curtain to reveal a well lit stage. Music began to play. It was some sort of performance. She stepped back to where a couch was placed facing the stage and seated herself, to see what would happen.

A play performed before her eyes. She forgot herself as soon as it began, and was wholly engrossed in the story. There were heroes and battles, and witches and curses, love and hatred, betrayal and fidelity, deception and honor. When the curtain fell at the end of it she was recalled to reality. Then only did she think to wonder if the actors were real people or simply illusions. If they were real people, could she talk to them?

She went again to the curtain, moving it aside with her arm to step behind it. But alas! There was now a wall there, and not a stage. She was further perturbed and disappointed when she realized she could not recall any detail of the story she had just seen. There had been a witch, she knew. But that had been such a small part of the story. Yet it was the witch that came clearest to her memory. Then she remembered as though she were hearing it again, the curse the witch had uttered:

> *Take heed, my sweet,*
> *For you shall rue*
> *The day you found*
> *In me a foe;*
>
> *And what, you ask,*
> *Is my revenge?*
> *You will not understand,*
> *But I will tell:*
>
> *To think you know*
> *When you know not;*
> *To think you see*
> *When you are blind;*
>
> *No might can break,*
> *No wit cast off,*
> *This curse with which*
> *I bind thee;*

Your cunning plans,
Your strength of will,
Alike shall fail
To free thee.

It can be broken, yes;
The way of that is hid;
You never shall break free,
As none before you did.

A lowly thing,
A gentle thing,
May break the spell at last;

But hope is vain
That wastes itself
On such a hopeless task.

It was like a riddle. What was the lowly, gentle thing that could break the spell? Why couldn't she remember?

Everything in the castle was so perplexing. It was that horrid beast's fault. If there were a curse, he was the one who had cast it, she was sure. He was probably trying to confuse her intentionally, so he could control her. He did want her to marry him after all, whatever his motive might be. It had occurred to her before that he must be some sort of nobleman to have such a grand castle. Now she was sure that he must have murdered the rightful owners and stolen their estate. She couldn't bear to see him again; she wouldn't.

That evening, when the floating candelabra entered her room to escort her to dinner, Beauty did not get up. Though she was not at all sure if there really was an invisible servant to hear her, nor what the consequences would be if there were, she held her head up high and said, "I will not be going to dinner this evening."

The candelabra withdrew. Beauty was left alone in her room, waiting for some repercussion. She thought perhaps this would be the defiance that incited the beast's wrath. Perhaps he would storm in and command her to the dining hall.

Half an hour passed with no occurrence. Could she just refuse dinner that easily? Of course, she must go to bed hungry, but it was a small price to pay, if she could avoid seeing the beast.

Another half an hour passed, and still nothing happened. She began to think that she would never have to dine with the beast again. As long as she ate plenty at teatimes, she would hardly suffer at all. Then she thought of her prince, and hoping she would dream of him again, decided to go to bed early.

Beauty did dream of her prince that night, but he was always far away from her, and whenever she tried to go to him, there was some wall, or mountain, or hedge, that kept him out of reach.

Seventh Chapter

For the next several days Beauty amused herself in her own rooms, and within those parts of the castle she had already explored. Each evening the candelabra would appear, and each evening she would refuse dinner, and the candelabra would withdraw. And each night she would dream that she was looking for her prince, but could not find him. Sometimes she thought she had found him, only to discover it was not him after all. Sometimes she could hear him calling to her on the wind, faint and distant, "Beauty..."

She would awake in the mornings disheartened, and lonely. Yet by the time night came again, she would go to bed with a renewed hope that this time at last the dream would be different and she would find her prince. Once she dreamed that a deep ravine separated her from her prince. An angry river raged at the bottom. Her prince beckoned to her, but she could see no way across.

Days became weeks. Life began to seem dull and unvarying. She seemed to forget that she had first come to the castle by her own choice. More and more she began to think of herself as a prisoner, and the beast as her cruel captor.

Much of her time she spent reading during daylight hours, and sometimes by candlelight, but always trying not to think too hard about the stories she read. She finished all the books on the shelves in her room. This drove her to spend more time wandering the gardens and grounds.

One day she struck upon a wide path paved with bluish stones. It took her across a lush green sward, and became an avenue, with high groomed hedges on either side. At last, she came to the gate. It was wrought of iron, at least thirty feet tall, and built into the living stone of a mighty rock face. It was of course the same gate by which her father had entered. But she did not know this.

She looked through and saw a thickly wooded slope descending into obscurity. All beyond the gate was shrouded in snow. Out there was beyond the beast's domain. Of course it would be locked. She put her hand to the latch. It was not locked. Her heart began to beat faster. She looked over her shoulder; the castle was not visible from where she stood. Perhaps this was her chance to escape. She could return to her father's house—see her family again. At the lightest touch, the gate swung open noiselessly. There was freedom before her. A chill gust smote her face like a warning. She hesitated. She seemed to hear the beast's voice in her head:

"Do not go, Beauty; the forest is treacherous and full of death."

Then she imagined the beast standing over the bloodied body of a poor creature he had just killed.

Nothing worse than what I leave behind, she thought, and stepped through the gate.

She was free. She thought she would have felt lighter, but instead her heart grew heavy. She tried to shake off the feeling, and began descending the slope. She had no idea which direction she ought to go, but she thought by choosing one and keeping to it, she was sure to come across some village or farmland eventually. And from there she could seek help and direction.

The trees were lovely in the snow, and she thoroughly enjoyed her walk, for several hours. Then the terrain became increasingly difficult. The underbrush grew more densely, the ground became more uneven, and the snow lay thicker upon it. Her toes grew numb, and then her feet. She began to worry. She was not dressed for a winter's night. She had only a light shawl to ward off the cold. She marched on with determined steps. Somehow she would manage. The idea that the beast was evil had rooted itself so securely in her mind that she would have rather died than go back to him.

That was while she could still feel her legs, and before she had felt any real hunger.

Night began to fall, and the air grew colder. She had never been alone in a forest at night before. Fear crept in, and was fed by the strange sounds and deceitful shadows which played around her. A wolf howled. It was far away. She decided she would have to keep walking through the night if she didn't want to freeze.

So walk she did.

Fortunately there was little wind. Somehow she made it through that terrible night. In the morning she was tired, and cold, and hungry, but alive. She rubbed and chafed her limbs to try to get some blood into them, ate some snow, and trudged on.

By the afternoon she was staggering with exhaustion and cold. She told herself it couldn't be much farther before she came to the end of the forest. Her family had traveled around it in two days after all. It couldn't take much longer than that to travel through it. At least, such were the reasonings of her feverish brain.

Hunger gnawed her from the inside. By the second nightfall she was too weak to go on or care what happened to her. She burrowed a little nest for herself in the snow, and slept.

Beauty was startled awake without knowing what woke her. It was still dark. Her blood pounded in her ears. She heard a snarling growl, and a pair of green eyes gleamed in the darkness, not twenty feet from her. Then she saw that there were many, many pairs of eyes, surrounding her in a semicircle. The occasional growls and snarls convinced her of their intent, had she any doubts.

A cloud moved off to reveal the moon; it shone down with an eerie light. She had never seen a wolf, but knew that these must be wolves. Falling asleep into the snowy arms of the forest was one way to die; being torn limb from limb as you scream in agony was another entirely. The wolves closed in on her slowly, as though savoring her terror, taunting her to run—as if she could.

Time slowed almost to a halt. She wished there were someone to save her. Her dream-prince, he would fight off the savage wolves and rescue her, if he were real. Then she thought of the beast. Yes, he had taken a life. He had never said why. She had never asked. Might not one kill because they are protecting one they love, and not because they enjoy killing?

At that moment, the forest was filled with a roar like that of a lion. Beauty's whole body trembled with the shock of it. She could not tell from whence it came, for it was all around her. The wolves immediately began to cower and whine in fear. Then Beauty felt a great shadow over her. She looked up and saw the terrible, shaggy form of the beast. He stood over her protectively, possessively, as if declaring to the wolves, "This is mine; touch her if you dare."

In the silence which followed the roar, the wolves resumed their hostile attitude. The leader of the pack growled low, sizing up the opposition. There was but one standing between him and his prey. Some communication must have passed between the leader and his pack, for the next moment the wolves rushed in as a body. The same moment the beast leapt to meet them. A cloud passed over the moon, and Beauty could not see what was happening, only confused shadows, punctuated with yelps, growls, and sounds of impact.

When the moon again shone out from behind the clouds, Beauty saw a silhouette of the beast's massive form standing over the dead alpha wolf. The rest of the wolves, seeing their leader dead, scattered into the trees. The fight was over.

Beauty tried to raise herself, but her limbs would not obey. Then she doubted whether her eyes were open or shut. She thought they were open, but all was darkness before them. Then she felt herself gently lifted from the snow, and lost consciousness completely.

Eighth Chapter

Beauty awoke in her own bed in the beast's castle. The image of the beast standing over the dead wolf was still clear in her mind. It was so similar to images her imagination had conjured in past weeks, yet so very different. The beast of her imaginings had been a heartless brute, and the beast of her memory was a fierce protector. The old longing stirred in her heart to uncover the mystery of the castle, and its master. Who was he, really? Her heart smote her for judging him based on her own presumptions. He had always been gentle toward her;

he had only shown her kindness. Yes, and more than kindness, for he honored her wishes and choices, even to his own hurt.

Did her actions hurt him? This was a new idea, and she was left to wonder.

The little gilt clock told her the morning was gone. She must have slept for hours, though it seemed only minutes before that she had lost consciousness. She was very hungry; breakfast was her next thought. And an uncommonly good one was spread for her.

It was not until after the edge was taken off her hunger that she first noticed she was not wearing the stained and torn dress of yesterday, but a clean nightgown of creamy whiteness.

She thought to examine her limbs for any lasting damage from the cold. There were no signs of frostbite anywhere. Someone had cared for her with great attention, and put her to bed. This brought the idea of invisible servants once more to mind.

Instead of dismissing the thought with a feeling of discomfort, as before, Beauty allowed her mind to venture down this path. If they were there, surely they could see and hear her. Were they human? It was rather alarming to consider that they might not be. She would imagine that they were human.

She suddenly remembered the beast saying upon her first arrival: *"If you are in want of anything, you have but to ask."*

Might this mean that she could speak to the servants and they would do her bidding? This was certainly a theory worth testing.

Beauty looked about the room; her eye fell on the iridescent rose. It still rested in the vase on the little table by her chair. She noticed for the first time that in all the weeks that she had been at the castle the rose had not even begun to wilt.

She went over to examine it more closely. It was as lovely and blooming as the day she had placed it there. Cupping the flower gently in her hand, she lowered her face toward it till her nose nearly touched the petals. She had always loved the smell of roses, but this rose surpassed all roses of her memory. Could she even call it a smell, when all her senses seemed to participate in the experience?

Now knowing what she would ask, she straightened and gave another glance around the room. It took her a moment to overcome the feeling of foolishness that came on her, but she said aloud to the empty room, "I would like to be shown the rose garden where this rose came from. If I may."

"Then I will lead you there, with pleasure, Mehr'u'tah." The voice was feminine, with a peculiar accent that Beauty could not place.

"Have you been there all the time, and silent?" Beauty asked.

"Not always silent, but you have been without the ability to hear until now."

"Oh." Beauty did not know what to make of this.

"Come," the voice said.

Beauty felt a hand grasp her own, gently but firmly.

"Oughtn't I to dress first?" Beauty asked.

"If you wish, Mehr'u'tah," the voice replied as the hand led her into her bedroom. "Shall I choose a dress for you, or would you like to choose yourself?"

"Oh, please choose one for me," Beauty said, as the hand let go of hers.

A dress was brought from the wardrobe, and Beauty was soon ready to venture outdoors. Once more the hand took hers, and led her out into the gardens through the portico adjoining her bedroom.

"Are you the one who put me to bed?" Beauty asked as they emerged from the sweet coolness within the tunnel of foliage and into the warm sunshine. A gentle breeze made the purple and yellow flowers sway and nod friendly greetings to each other.

"Yes," the voice replied. "But it was the Master who restored your blood."

"Restored my blood?" This was altogether strange and unsettling.

"To reverse the damage of the forest."

"How did he do that?"

"As only he can."

"You called him 'the Master'?"

"That is one of his names; he has many," the voice said.

"If he has so many names, I wonder that I know none of them."

"You will. It matters little what you call him, so long as you let him define the name, and not the name define him."

Beauty thought that surely the name she had given him in her own thoughts—'the beast'—would not be well received if spoken aloud. "What should I call him?" she asked.

"I cannot tell you. That is between you and him."

"What am I to call you, then?"

"You may call me Nasira."

"It will be nice to have someone to talk to." Beauty looked over to where she assumed Nasira walked beside her. "Even if I can't see you. I have so many questions about the castle."

"I will not be able to answer very many of those," Nasira replied.

"Why not?"

"Many of those things which you have questions about, cannot be answered in the ordinary way. If I were to give you an answer, then you would think that you knew the answer, and it would only delay your true understanding."

Beauty thought about this, and did not reply.

Not long after, they came to a stone arch covered in green vines and delicate blue flowers. A golden plaque stood to one side of it, with the elegantly engraved warning that her father had chosen not to heed. She stopped a moment to read it, and Nasira let go of her hand.

> *Let this garden be for the pleasure of all who enter;*
> *Yet not one bud may be removed without consent.*
> *He who disregards this,*
> *His life is forfeit.*

"Why is it such a serious thing to take a flower from this garden?" Beauty asked.

"It is not always for us to understand; sometimes

all that is required is obedience," Nasira replied, still close beside her. "Go in, if you wish."

Beauty entered the rose garden with some hesitation, feeling strangely that she was intruding into someone's privacy. Whose privacy she did not think deeply enough to consider. After a few steps the feeling changed. She no longer felt like an intruder; she belonged here. There was still a definite feeling of peaceful seclusion; this was a secret garden. She somehow knew that Nasira had stayed outside. She was alone—alone with the garden. Or perhaps, alone with something Else that was in the garden. She wandered along the path, circling the fountain, enjoying the scent that the roses gave. The water of the fountain played an enchantingly sweet sort of music; Beauty had never known that water could sound so beautiful.

She found a bench at the far end of the garden, with roses growing up in a canopy over it. She sat there, and lost all track of time, as she rested, and breathed, and listened.

Suddenly, she thought of dinner, with an entirely new excitement. She stood, wondering if it was too early to dress. And then wondering if Nasira was still waiting outside the archway.

"Nasira, are you there?" Beauty asked, as she passed out of the rose garden.

"I am here," came the reply.

"Sorry to have kept you waiting."

"Waiting is not unpleasant to me; you need not apologize, Mehr'u'tah."

"Is it too early to dress for dinner, do you think?" Beauty asked.

"I think not, if you wish to." Nasira's smile could be heard in her voice.

Beauty spent a very enjoyable time getting ready for dinner that day. She talked with Nasira the whole time, as the servant assisted her.

A dark green gown was settled on. It had a richness about it, but was very simple in its design, with just a touch of embroidery, here and there, in gold.

At Nasira's offer, Beauty sat for her hair to be braided and arranged in an elegant manner. Nasira proved quite skillful in this art, and as Beauty surveyed the final result in her glass, she was convinced her hair had never looked more beautiful.

Her only adornment was a delicate sprig of white
flowers, with dark green leaves, which Nasira had secured
amid the woven locks of hair. Beauty thought her attire
suited her nature more than anything else she had ever
worn.

The anticipated knock on the door came. When the
floating candelabra appeared, Beauty ventured to say,
"Good evening."

"Good evening," a deep voice from behind the
candelabra spoke. "I am come to show you to dinner,
Mehr'u'tah."

"I am ready," Beauty replied.

As she entered the grand dining hall, and crossed its
green and white marble floor, she saw the beast standing
in his usual place by the head of the table, awaiting her. At
the sight of him, she could not help the chill fear that
gripped her, as with a physical giant hand. His exterior
was so terrifying. But she would not let the fear control
her; she kept her steps steady. The beast made a slight
bow as she came up, and she responded with a small
curtsy before taking her seat.

There was a brief silence between them, as the first
course was placed on the table. For once, Beauty was the
one to initiate conversation. "In all the time that I've been
here, I have not learnt your name. What am I to call you?"

He hummed audibly, as though thinking. "You may call me..." he paused. "Beast," he finished, most unexpectedly.

Beauty looked up into his face in her surprise. Their eyes met, and she thought she caught a playful glint in his. But surely she was mistaken. Her shock at his knowledge of the epithet she had given him in her secret thoughts, was quickly followed by profound bewilderment that it did not offend him.

He added, "At least, until you come across another name you find suits me better."

My Savior. The thought came immediately to Beauty's mind, but she was too timid to say it aloud. "Surely you have a proper name?" she persisted.

"I do. And someday you will know it."

Beauty found that if she looked into his eyes, his face was not so terrible.

"I'm sorry that I ran away. And I'm sorry for thinking wrongly of you."

"I know," he said gently—nay, tenderly.

Beauty did not know what to make of this tenderness, so she turned her attention to her plate. After a time of silence, she suddenly thought of the rose garden.

"I found the rose garden today," she said eagerly, looking up into his eyes once more. "Or, that is, Nasira showed it to me."

"I know," the Beast said again, this time with a smile. "What did you think of it?"

"I think it is my favorite place."

The Beast was pleased, but did not reply.

There was another natural pause in the conversation. Beauty's thoughts reverted to the subject of what name or title might suit the Beast.

"Are you a nobleman?" she asked.

"You might call me that."

"Are you going to make me guess?"

The Beast answered with silence, but his eyes invited questions.

"A baron?" Beauty asked.

"Not a baron."

"A duke?"

"Not a duke."

For the rest of dinner, Beauty went on to guess every title of ranked nobility she could think of, in every language she knew. But the reply was the same for all, occasionally emphasized by a shake of his great shaggy head.

"So you are not of the nobility?" Beauty asked again, when she could think of no more noble titles.

"No king appointed me, and no ancestor died,

to make me what I am."

For a fleeting moment, the old thought returned that perhaps he had killed the rightful owners of the estate, and was a usurper. But she did not believe that to be true. He seemed to be teasing her with his riddles. She was rather enjoying it, though. Her own playfulness rose to match his.

"Well," Beauty said at last, "I think I shall call you 'my lord,' even if you are not a duke or an earl. It seems fitting, since you do own such a grand estate, with such a castle as this."

"And here I had hoped you would have kept calling me 'Beast'."

"I shall spare 'Beast' for special occasions," Beauty ventured to tease. "By the way," she added, "how many rooms does this castle have? I've been into dozens and dozens of them, but I'm sure there are more that I've yet to see—I would not venture to guess how many."

"There are more than you will ever see, though you were to spend all your time exploring. You will find new wings and new levels each time you look for them, but you will never have reached the end, or seen all. You see, the castle is ever expanding."

"Oh! How mysterious. And marvelous! I've never heard sounds of building. But then I could not even hear your servants until just today. Is it being built by the invisible servants, or does the castle grow on its own like a living thing?"

"That is a very good question."

There was a long pause before Beauty realized that that was the only answer she was going to get.

Dinner was concluded; they both rose from their seats. In that moment, it flashed upon Beauty that he might ask her again to marry him. Her fear had long since vanished, but the idea made her feel rather uncomfortable.

Surely enough, he asked the question: "Beauty, will you be my wife?"

"No, my lord," she replied, looking down at the hem of her dress.

"Then I bid you goodnight."

"Goodnight, my lord."

That awkwardness was over.

In the privacy of her own bedroom, Nasira helped her off with her things, and took down her hair. Beauty's thoughts were occupied with the vastness of the castle, and its bewildering expansion. She decided she would have to spend the morrow exploring. Then she thought of her dream-prince, and was eager to go to bed.

"Goodnight, Mehr'u'tah," Nasira said, as Beauty

pulled the soft blankets over herself.

"Goodnight," Beauty replied. As she laid her head on the pillows, a thought struck her. "Nasira, why do you call me Mehr-u-tah? What does it mean?"

"It means: Beloved of the King," Nasira answered, and then the door shut behind her.

"The King..." Beauty murmured, already half asleep. "What king?"

Thoughts of kings soon vanished from her head, replaced by thoughts of a prince. For the first time in many weeks, she dreamed that her prince was standing right in front of her, looking deeply into her eyes. There was no chasm or angry river between them. Then, the most beautiful music began to play from somewhere. He took her hand, slipped his arm around her waist, and they danced.

Ninth Chapter

It was between breakfast and teatime the following afternoon. Beauty was walking along a corridor, with windows of stained glass all along one side; daylight shone through and made colorful patterns on the floor and opposite wall. She was sure she had never been in this wing of the castle before. In another minute, she was standing before large double doors of carved ebony. The door handles were wrought iron, in the shape of outspread wings—they might have been eagle wings, or raven wings.

When Beauty opened one side of the door, the smell of faint wood smoke, aged leather, ink, and musty pages sent a thrill to her heart. She knew before her eyes could confirm it: she had found the library.

She stepped forward, feeling immediately at peace and in awe. The room was enormous, and lined floor to ceiling with books. Her first sweeping glance revealed this, as well as the ornate fireplaces, one at either end of the room. Above each fireplace was an elaborate wood-carving. Several lamps hung from an arched ceiling. These were unlike any Beauty had ever seen. Each lamp was like elegantly draped gossamer, glowing softly, and yet somehow sending light into every corner of the library. As far as Beauty could tell, the glowing gossamer was supported by a frame of decorative wrought iron.

There were mezzanines around portions of the room, each one accessed by a winding staircase with wrought iron railings. In other portions of the room, there was no perceivable way to access the upper shelves.

Beauty began slowly walking along one wall, her gaze vaguely wandering over the beautifully bound volumes that filled the shelves. She very soon realized that the room was not as it had first appeared. There were secret nooks, and recesses, where one could hide away to enjoy a book. Some were obscured by a curtain, some only obscured by the wall they receded into. Some had large cushions for a seat, some had chairs. Some were little more than a nook, others were small rooms. After some investigation, Beauty was convinced that there were at least twelve hide-aways, where solitary readers could be occupied, their presence entirely unknown to one just entering the room. There were also comfortable chairs placed near both fireplaces, if one preferred.

Toward the middle of the room, a long table was covered with many and various maps. Another table was covered with star-charts, and other instruments of which Beauty did not know the use. She glanced over the maps and charts for a few minutes, but could make neither head nor tail of them, and soon returned to the bookshelves.

Once more she wandered slowly around the perimeter of the room, this time stopping frequently to run her fingers gently over the bindings, occasionally pulling one out to read its title. If the title interested her, she would open the boards—almost reverently—and glance over the opening lines. Some of these she placed back on the shelves, but some she tucked under her arm to be taken back to her room.

When she had collected upwards of half a dozen volumes, she decided to take them into one of the cozy nooks and read there for a while. Some of the more spacious hide-aways had their own hanging gossamer lamp. Beauty chose one that also had a large painting in it. The painting was like a window looking out over a garden, and it was so life-like, that she felt she may as well have been sitting at a real window. It reminded her vaguely of what had been her favorite reading nook back in the old house in Florens. So there she settled, upon a wonderfully comfortable cushioned seat below the painting.

As she looked over the books she had gathered, and chose which to begin first, she thought how nice it would be if her rooms were closer to the library. She glanced up absently before immersing herself in the chosen book, and then momentarily forgot about the book in her hand. There was a small door in this nook that she had not noticed before. Intrigued, she got up to investigate. It looked like it might be only a closet. She could not imagine what it might contain. She tried the latch. It opened readily, but she could see nothing. Another moment and she realized there was a tapestry obscuring the doorway. She swept it aside with her arm, and stood stunned.

It was her own room. The tapestry was one she looked at every day, without any idea that there was a door behind it. But how? She was in an entirely different wing of the castle—at least a ten minute walk from her rooms. She stepped through the door, letting the tapestry fall back in front of it. This was definitely her room. There was the fire blazing, and her chair, and the little table with her rose in its porcelain vase. She pushed aside the tapestry again and stepped back through the door. There was the pile of books awaiting her on the cushioned seat where she had left them, and just beyond, the library. Had it been there, adjoining her room, all the time? Or had it moved because she wished it? That was absurd! ...wasn't it?

As baffling and mysterious as this discovery was, Beauty did not let it distract her for very long. Soon she was curled up on the cushioned seat below the window-painting, absorbed in the pages of a new story.

At dinner that evening Beauty found she had much to talk about. She forgot to count the courses, so engaged was she in the conversation.

The lord of the castle did not seem to mind her loquacious mood, nor did he seem lost when she wandered from one subject to another, apparently unconnected. Once or twice Beauty began to fear she was rambling incoherently, but the Beast would interject, or ask a question that opened the thought even further than she had taken it, and she knew he understood her.

The last course was finished, but Beauty did not notice. The conversation went on, flowing from one thing to another, until she found herself sharing memories of her own childhood, and confiding things she had never told another soul.

After some time, there was a lull in the conversation, and she became aware of the empty plates, and the lateness of the hour. Suddenly self-conscious, she remained silent.

Then the Beast stood, and asked her, as she now expected, "Beauty, will you be my wife?"

The proposal no longer made her uneasy. There was even an indefinite smile as she replied, "No, my lord."

He bid her a good night, and she was escorted back to her room by the holder of the candelabra.

It was not until Nasira had left her for the night that Beauty began to feel amazement at her own conduct. She was not usually so talkative. In fact, she despised "prattlers." The Beast had not talked about himself at all, yet she had gone on and on talking about herself.

Was she the very thing she despised? Was she only quiet in other company—even the company of her own sisters—because she feared being scorned? Perhaps she feared to be misunderstood.

In other company, she had always a conviction that her thoughts were too deep for her listeners, so she kept most of them to herself. Was this another evidence of pride, that most deceitful of vices? The Beast made her feel that her "deep thoughts" were only shallow after all, and there was much she had yet to learn and uncover.

She fell asleep wondering if it was possible for a person to view themselves without prejudice. She thought not. But if not, was there any hope of truly knowing oneself?

These thoughts colored and disturbed her dreams. First she dreamt she was wandering in the streets of a great city, teeming with people. She was pushed and shoved and trod upon; no one seemed to see her at all. Then suddenly the dream changed and she was alone in a room of mirrors. Her reflection was repeated in all the facets around her. To her horror, she was nothing but a featureless blank. These sorts of impossible things do happen in dreams: she *saw* as with eyes that she had no eyes. Panic gripped her. Then again the dream changed and she was in a wide open meadow. Her prince was standing amid white and purple flowers. He took her gently by the shoulders and looked deeply into her eyes. The panic and fear faded away. He spoke, and his words were full of comfort:

"You need not be known to yourself, to be known by another."

Beauty awoke with a physical ache in her chest; she desired to be known. What good was the comfort of a dream-prince anyway? It only made waking up alone the more painful. She realized she had always ached to be known—though she had never identified the ache before, it had always been there, buried.

She dressed, and ate her breakfast in dejected silence.

"Is something wrong?" Nasira asked with sincere concern.

Beauty wanted to tell Nasira how she felt, but as she thought how to begin, she became overwhelmed. How could she attempt to communicate what she had no words for?

"I'm fine," she said instead. "Just a little sad."

In that moment, the ache dulled, and she felt more than ever that she could never articulate it. This was her habit, bury the ache. The numbness, seeping and muting, was just as bad as the ache itself. She did not want to be numb, but she did not know how to stop the invasion of numbness.

"I have something to show you then." Nasira took her hand.

"You don't have to cheer me up," Beauty replied.

"This is not 'to cheer you up'."

Nasira led her through the castle to a room with high arched ceilings, and beautiful wood paneling. The architecture of the room was clearly for acoustic perfection, not merely aesthetic appeal. It was filled with more musical instruments than Beauty could name.

"You may come here to play these instruments anytime you wish, and..." Nasira led her to a door at the far end of the room before releasing her hand. The moment Nasira opened this door, the sounds of an orchestra met Beauty's ear from beyond it. "If you do not feel like playing yourself," Nasira continued, "you can simply listen."

Beauty entered the concert hall and sat. It mattered not that the musicians were invisible to her; it was enough that she could hear.

She thought—or imagined—that the song changed when she entered. It was a sad song. The individual notes of the intricate harmonies pierced her heart; tears filled her eyes. Then one instrument soared above the rest in a wailing solo, and her heart broke open. Sobs convulsed her body. The ache she had buried was embodied in the song—or perhaps the song stripped away her walls and laid it bare. She knew not how long she wept, as the song of yearning played on.

At last her tears were spent, and the song became more gentle, with sweeter notes of hope lifting her above the melancholy. The ache had subsided. It was not like the dullness she was used to, but like there had been a wound that was cleaned, and could now heal. A seed had been planted in her heart, eradicating the bitter root of unfulfilled desire with the calm expectancy of its eventual fruition. She continued to sit, peacefully listening for quite some time.

When she finally did leave the concert hall, she felt fresh and washed, like a meadow after rainfall.

The music room, where she had left Nasira, seemed different than before—strangely more alive. It was almost as though each instrument *desired* to be played, and was silently asking to be taken up. There was an almost tangible expectancy about the whole room. Beauty silently promised to return on some future day and play some of them, but for now she was feeling surprisingly hungry. She asked Nasira what time it was.

"Almost teatime."

"Teatime! I was gone for that many hours? I would have guessed it had only been one! It is amazing how we can experience the passage of time as fast or slow, though time itself never changes."

"True," Nasira replied. "Our perceptions do not influence reality, only our own experience of it."

They returned to Beauty's rooms and found, surely enough, tea was spread invitingly on the table.

As she sunk her teeth into a buttered scone, Beauty thought it tasted even better than usual. And she was also quite convinced, a few moments later, that the jam was the best she'd ever had.

"Nasira, what kind of berry is this jam made from?"

"Whortleberries."

"Do they grow on the castle grounds somewhere?"

"They do. In the meadow beyond the orchards."

"I didn't know there were orchards!"

"Would you like to go berry-picking some afternoon?"

"Can we?" Beauty's face beamed. "I would like that very much. Is there time to go today?"

"I think it would be better to plan an entire afternoon

for the excursion," Nasira replied. "Besides, it is raining just now."

"Raining?" Beauty fairly jumped from her seat in her excitement. "This is the first time it's rained that I've been here!"

She immediately thought of the aviary, with its magnificent roof of domed glass. She had not been there since the day she had first discovered it.

"I'm going to the aviary," Beauty announced over her shoulder as she made her way to the door of her apartment. "I'll be back in time to dress for dinner!"

Nasira laughed. "I will have a dress laid out for you upon your return."

"Thank you!" Beauty called back as she was shutting the door behind herself.

She set off down the passage, and did not pause till she reached the aviary. Though the way was quite far from her rooms, through many doors and corridors of various descriptions, and up and down several stairs of differing heights, Beauty found she remembered every turn perfectly. Now and then, she could distinguish the soft pattering of the rain on the distant castle roof.

At length, she stood before the arched door of the aviary. There was an image of a bird actually carved into the door, which had escaped her notice the last time.

As on her first visit, when she entered, she was met by the sound of countless bird voices all singing in surprising harmony. This time they were accompanied by the pleasant thrumming of the rain upon the glass dome overhead.

The abundance of unusual plants and foliage gave everything a green and tranquil aspect. Beauty walked along the winding path until she stood directly under the center of the dome. The rain drops spattered and made runnels along the glass, and the runnels converged, and split, making unpredictable patterns. It was even more beautiful than she had imagined it would be. But the sound was best of all.

Presently, her notice was drawn to a branch a few feet from her. She immediately recognized Little Red, with his persistent chirping, seeking her attention, as usual. When he saw she was looking, he bowed repeatedly and chirped. Then he cocked his head to one side and chirped again. For some reason, Beauty no longer found his tenacious personality to be annoying. She put out her hand to him, and he flew up to perch on her finger without hesitation.

"You are very bold, aren't you?" Beauty asked rhetorically.

Little Red just looked at her with his head cocked to one side for a moment. Then he set about rearranging one or two feathers with his beak, which were apparently out of place.

Beauty smiled. "Oh you needn't fuss on my account."

Little Red looked up and began chattering in earnest.

"You certainly have a lot to say."

He bobbed his head up and down dramatically, chirping all the while.

Beauty laughed.

Suddenly, a little grey bird with red under her wings flew up and landed nearby. The red under her wings disappeared when she folded them. There was a red stripe like a collar on her neck, and a few red feathers in her tail. She chirruped sweetly.

"This is your wife, I suppose. A pleasure to meet you, Madam."

Little Red flew from Beauty's hand to perch beside the little grey bird. They both looked at Beauty, and then Little Red flew to a branch a little ways down the path. A few moments later, his mate flew to a branch even further down the path. They both turned back to look at Beauty again. It was clear they wanted her to follow them. When they saw she was coming, they flew a few more feet and stopped to wait. In this manner, she was led toward one of the corners of the quadrangle. They reached a small tree with enormous leaves of dark green.

"Oh! Is this your nest?" Beauty approached slowly. "I've never seen anything like it. It's a perfect little basket. Did you weave it all yourself?"

Little Red twittered pragmatically and puffed out his chest.

"What a clever bird you are!"

After she had sufficiently admired his nest, Little Red seemed utterly disinterested in her. Beauty was amused by the sudden change.

Seeing that he was done with her attentions, she turned to explore the rest of the aviary.

Some of the birds were content to observe her from a distance, while others ignored her entirely, and still others were more curious and amiable. Beauty was befriended by a sapphire-blue bird, with a creamy yellow breast, and a pure white bird with small black eyes. There was a green bird with a yellow head, and a yellow bird with a black tail. This last had a charming little warble to his voice.

A certain black bird with blue and green wings made Beauty laugh out loud. He had a trick of pointing his beak straight up at the sky when he sang, and then shaking his head vigorously when his song ended.

There were beautiful golden flowers that grew on a vine high overhead. Beauty was admiring them, when the sapphire-blue bird suddenly flew up and plucked one with his beak. He brought it to Beauty as a gift.

"Oh, thank you, how kind! The petals are so lovely, with these delicate fringes. Reminds me of lace."

When he saw that she was pleased, the bird returned to pluck another, and kept bringing them to her until she had a small bunch in her hand.

"Another one?" Beauty laughed as the eighth blossom was given to her. "I think this is plenty, thank you. Perhaps I shall ask Nasira to put them in my hair."

She raised the blossoms to her nose; they had a sweet, crisp scent, not unlike honeysuckle.

Beauty sighed contentedly. She found a little stone seat, and sat for a while, just watching and listening to the birds and the rain.

Beauty entered the dining hall that evening wearing a cream colored dress, with the golden flowers in her hair. The Beast greeted her as usual. When they were seated, the Beast noticed the golden flowers and said, "I see you have been to the aviary."

"Yes, my lord," Beauty replied, smiling as she used the epithet. "It is so nice there, when the rain is playing on the roof. Though I believe the rain has stopped now."

"And did you find the birds entertaining? I always do," the Beast chuckled.

"Yes, I did." Beauty's smile broadened. She proceeded to relate in great detail all of her encounters with the various birds she had befriended, from the persistence and vanity of Little Red, to the obliging generosity of the sapphire-blue bird, whom she had nicknamed Gentian. The Beast seemed to enjoy listening to her, and was amused by the birds' antics.

"When I got up to leave, there was Gentian with one final flower as a parting gift," Beauty said, coming to the end of her story. "Nasira was kind enough to put them in my hair for me."

"They look well there," the Beast said.

Soon after that, Beauty mentioned in passing her visit to the concert hall, but didn't go into any of the particulars. The experience was too personal. She was not used to speaking of such things. And she was shy of exposing such intimate emotions to the mysterious "Lord of the Castle."

So she quickly moved on to Nasira's suggestion of going out to the meadow to pick whortleberries.

"You should take the summer carriage," the Beast offered.

Beauty paused with a bite of food halfway to her mouth. "The summer carriage?"

She suddenly realized there must be horses kept somewhere on the estate. And then felt foolish for never having thought of it before. Of course there were horses! There had been horses pulling the carriage that first brought her to the castle.

"This may seem foolish," Beauty confessed, "but I never thought of the fact that you must keep horses until this minute."

"Perhaps you would enjoy going out to the pasture with me some morning."

This suggestion rather startled Beauty. Spend time with him apart from dinner? She had compartmentalized him quite nicely to that single time of day, and it made her uncomfortable to think of seeing him at any other time. But meeting the horses was somewhat tempting.

"Perhaps some morning," Beauty replied vaguely.

Dinner concluded in its usual manner; the proposal was made and refused.

As she prepared for bed that night, Beauty mentioned the summer carriage to Nasira, and asked if it was possible to go berry-picking the following day.

"Of course," Nasira replied. "If the Master offered the summer carriage, it will be ready when it is wanted."

"You will be coming with me, won't you?" Beauty asked.

"Yes, I will come," Nasira assured her. "If you like, I will make arrangements to bring a picnic," the servant added. "That way, we need not rush back for tea, and may enjoy the afternoon at leisure."

Beauty was very pleased with this idea, and everything was soon decided.

She went to bed feeling like a child on the eve of a holiday, full of joyous expectation for the morrow.

Tenth Chapter

By eleven o'clock the next morning, Beauty was standing in a paved courtyard, equipped with a large hat, its purple ribbons tied prettily under her chin, and an empty basket, destined to be filled with whortleberries. There was a large stone arch at either end of the courtyard, and a small fountain at its center. On the near side of this fountain stood an elegant summer carriage, with a pair of grey horses in the harness, who seemed as eager to start as Beauty herself.

Without even pausing to think how odd it was, Beauty

gave the invisible coachman a cheerful, "Good morning!"

He replied with a deep and throaty, "Good morning!"

"I've brought a few apple pieces to give the horses, if that's alright?" Beauty asked.

"Of course, Mehr'u'tah!" was the gruff reply.

With this encouragement, Beauty went around to greet the horses. She stroked their velvety noses, and told them they were beauties, and gave them the apple pieces she had brought.

When she went to step into the carriage, there was an invisible helping hand right where she needed it. She wondered if it was Nasira, or the coachman, or perhaps a footman who had not spoken, but was too shy to ask.

After Beauty was seated in the carriage, with Nasira across from her, the coachman spoke again—even with its gruff quality, his voice was kind. "Would you prefer to go the long way around, or more directly to the meadow?"

"Oh, the long way, please!" Beauty replied.

The horses started at once. They passed out of the courtyard by one of the arches, and entered a wide avenue bordered with evergreen hedges. From this, they turned into a second avenue, where the trees on either side of them had mottled trunks of pale and dark grey, and rounded leaves that were almost more blue than green. The spreading branches cast a partial shade over the path. One branch hung down lower than the rest. Beauty reached up as they passed under it, and the low-hanging leaves just brushed her fingertips.

At the end of this avenue was another stone arch, larger than the first, and covered with creeping vines. Beyond the arch, they came upon a large open square, paved with red and white stones. A great fountain stood at the center. In the midst of the fountain was a statue of a winged lion, the water flowing over its outstretched wings, and cascading into the pool below. Enormous stone statues stood prominently all around the square, like sentinels guarding the open space. The effect was striking. At first Beauty thought the statues were of giant men in robes, but she soon noticed that they had the heads of eagles.

She asked Nasira about them, but the answer only left more questions.

Next they came to a tiered flower garden. It was more wild-looking than most of the castle gardens Beauty had seen. The flowers were arranged so that as they drove along, they passed from color to color. At first it was all yellow flowers, changing shade by shade to orange, and then pink, deepening gradually to burgundy, and so on. This spectrum of flowers went on for a considerable distance, ending with dark blue. The carriage then entered a grove of birch trees, with the dark blue flowers spilling over from the tiered flowerbeds onto the woodland floor of the grove, looking more wild than ever.

Beauty caught sight of a small creature, somewhat resembling a badger, standing up on its hind legs among the trees. The creature had evidently paused in its important task of eating to watch her pass; there was no fear in its small black eyes, only curiosity.

They emerged from the grove onto golden barley fields, stretching away into the distance on either side of their path. The coachman observed that the color of the fields, and the droop of the barley-heads, indicated that the barley was nearly ready for harvest.

Beyond the fields was open countryside; the road wound gently between green hills covered in purple heather. The singing of a thrush drew Beauty's attention heavenward. A few cumulus clouds were scattered across the deep blue sky. The bird flew in a graceful arc, and then descended to land amidst the heather. The thrush was not the only creature drawn to the heather; there were dozens—perhaps hundreds—of brightly colored butterflies flitting here and there among blossoms.

Beauty could not see much of where their road was taking them, because of the hilly terrain, but she did espy other moorland creatures as they drove along.

Most of these creatures were of kinds she had never before seen. She kept pointing to different ones and asking Nasira what they were called.

At length, the carriage rounded one of the many hills, and a treeline came into view.

"All of these lands belong to your master?" Beauty marveled.

"And you have only seen a small piece yet," Nasira replied.

"You did say you wanted to go the long way," the coachman chuckled.

"I'm not complaining!" Beauty laughed. "It's all so beautiful!"

They entered a forest of towering elm trees, making a dense canopy high overhead. Deeper into the woodland, there were oak and ash trees mixed with the elms. Beauty saw a herd of deer grazing serenely. The old stag raised his crowned head to watch the carriage, but evidently did not consider them a threat.

Beauty could hear the babbling of a brook long before she caught sight of it. Then for some time, the brook's course more or less followed them, occasionally winding away out of sight, but more often flowing just beside their path. They eventually crossed over it on a wooden bridge, after which they seemed to leave it behind, and its song was soon lost among the trees.

They crossed a glade full of red and white daisies, where a family of rabbits was scampering and playing. No sooner was the carriage again surrounded by trees, then Beauty heard once more the sound of flowing waters, no longer a gentle babble, but a distant thundering. She wondered if it was the same brook that had found them again, or a different one. The forest floor became more uneven around them, though their road was smooth, and Beauty could not see the water, though its noise steadily increased.

All at once, the waterfall came into view; she caught her breath and exclaimed aloud at the beauty of it. The water made a white pattern over the rocks as it fell and foamed into a pool of emerald green. Beauty turned in her seat to gaze at it longer, and the coachman proved his attentiveness by stopping the carriage without a word. They sat for several minutes enjoying the scene. No one tried to speak above the waterfall's sonorous music.

When the horses started again, their road turned sharply, and they entered beneath a natural arch of rock. Here the road divided into two ways. One led up toward the dark opening of a cavern in the side of a mossy rock face; Beauty thought she heard the distant sounds of miners working away in the depths.

The horses took the other way, leading into a shallow canyon. Along the top of the canyon there were many figures, which Beauty took to be statues of colored glass. They caught and refracted the light into rainbows on the floor of the canyon. She was startled when one of them took to the air, and she realized it was a living creature with wings.

"What are they?" Beauty asked in amazement.

"They are called Cuarinak," Nasira replied.

"I've never seen anything like them!"

Just then one of the Cuarinak whistled, high and clear as a flute. Another Cuarinak whistled out a different note, and then a third and fourth Cuarinak, each with their own note, in a descending arpeggio. After that there was a pause, like at a concert when the musicians have tuned their instruments and are ready to begin. Beauty barely had time to wonder if there would be more, when the quartet began. In four part harmony, as if they were reading from sheet music, the Cuarinak sang. Their song echoed through the canyon, and concluded just as the carriage was leaving it.

Beauty brushed a tear off her cheek. "Their song was so beautiful and joyful, I don't know why I'm crying."

"Hope is a mysterious thing," Nasira said. "Joy and longing joined together."

"Yes, that's it; their song perfectly embodied hope," Beauty replied. "Hope of what though?"

Her musing question remained unanswered, and she was soon distracted by the changing scenery.

The carriage came into a lane of ancient willows, their branches trailing down to the earth. A gentle breeze stirred the willow tendrils.

"Was that a door I just saw in the trunk of that willow?" Beauty asked suddenly.

"Yes. Some of the groundskeepers live in this avenue."

Beauty was left to wonder what sort of creatures the groundskeepers were.

Finally, the lane of willows opened onto the meadow. It was a large grassy expanse, sprinkled with purple and white flowers. Beauty thought it looked strangely familiar. Why did it feel like she had been here before?

The orchards began at the far side of the meadow, separated from it by a low fence. Beauty could not ascertain the extent of the orchards from her vantage. Obscuring the bottom portion of the fence, was the dense growth of berry bushes that was their destination. The low bushes followed the fence line invariably, but more wild-looking than a hedge.

As they crossed the meadow, she suddenly realized why it seemed so familiar.

"I think I dreamt of this place the other night!"

"I wouldn't doubt it," was Nasira's reply.

"And there was—" Beauty stopped. She didn't want to mention her dream-prince, so she quickly came up with something else to say instead. "There were purple and white flowers just like these ones, and every rise and dip of ground was just the same. But how could I have dreamt of a place I had never been?"

"One would have to understand a great deal about what a dream is before they could venture to answer that question."

"Here we are!" the coachman announced, as the carriage rolled to a stop not ten paces from the line of whortleberry bushes.

Again, the invisible hand helped Beauty out of the carriage. She was fairly certain that it was the coachman, but received no confirmation of this, for he did not reply to her thanks.

Beauty wasted no time in attacking the berry bushes. With her basket on her arm, and her hat shading her head and neck, she bent over the bushes, picking those berries that seemed good to her. Unaware was she of the graceful picture she made. Now and then a berry was taken up to her mouth rather than dropped into her basket. But such is almost a rule with berry-picking.

At first she chatted intermittently with Nasira as she picked, but soon fell to her own thoughts as she gradually worked her way further from the carriage.

After a long silence, she observed, "No matter how many I pick, my basket doesn't seem to grow heavier, and there always seems room for more."

"A mystery indeed," said a voice that was not Nasira's. "The *logical* conclusion would be a hole in the basket."

Beauty turned toward the speaker, and saw a little man sitting on the fence above the berry bushes. He had a long black beard, and a great big nose, and green eyes that twinkled at her. Beauty lifted her basket to examine the bottom of it, but all was as it should be.

The little man laughed. "Then again, things hereabouts don't bend to 'logic'—for logic is limited by understanding. Where understanding is incomplete, logic must fail."

"Why, I can see you!" Beauty exclaimed, as this realization struck her.

"Can you," the little man said, but it was not a question. His eyes twinkled all the more, and though his mouth was obscured by whiskers, there were crinkles of merriment around his eyes.

"I would ask why I can see you when I cannot see Nasira, but I'm sure you will say there is no logical explanation." Beauty was finding his merriment catching.

"Careful, little one; 'tis always dangerous to assume you know the answer before you've asked the question."

Beauty could not help laughing at this epithet he assigned her, fully appreciating the irony of it, for he was less than half her size.

"Well, why can I see you, then, when I cannot see Nasira, nor the coachman?" Beauty asked.

"I'm a simple chap."

"Well, that's no answer at all."

The dwarf only grinned through his eyes.

"What are you, anyway?" Beauty asked.

"I'm a groundskeeper."

"Oh! Do you live in the willow-tree house that I saw?"

"Very likely."

"What's your name?"

"Boeli."

"Bowl-ee?"

"Close enough."

Beauty cocked her head, still holding her basket, but not actively picking berries. "Are there many of you? Groundskeepers I mean."

"Oh yes, quite a lot of us. But not all are like me. Different types of grounds require different types of keepers."

"I see." There was a pause. Beauty had a sudden thought. "Maybe you can tell me how I could have dreamed of this place before I ever came here."

"I'm afraid not." Boeli gave a little chuckle. "Haven't the foggiest idea. The Master would know," he added.

"Oh." There was another pause. "Would you like to join us for our picnic?" Beauty invited, gesturing back toward the carriage.

"No, but I thank you. I must be getting along with my work."

Beauty thought that he spoke of his work as a person might speak of a holiday, with cheerful expectation of great pleasure. She looked out once more across the meadow, with its mottling of white and purple flowers standing out against its gently waving grasses; wild-looking as it was, she thought she could descry an artistic intentionality about it. When she turned again to the fence, Boeli was gone. Nor did she catch sight of him again for the rest of the afternoon.

When it was time to drive back, they took the shorter way, through the orchards. Beauty sat staring out across the perfect lines that the rows and columns of trunks made as they drove through acre after acre of fruit trees. The rows stretched away on either side of them as far as she could see. The sun was low in the sky, and the shadows stretched long.

"What a pleasant afternoon this has been!" Beauty sighed contentedly, and said no more for the rest of the drive. She was tired enough to prefer the peaceful silence over conversation. But a serene smile lit her face as the rays of the setting sun fell upon it.

At dinner that evening, Beauty told the Beast all about her day, things she had seen and done, and wondered about. And she listened with great interest, as he showed her many a shrouded mystery, and lifted the smallest corner of its shroud for her. She did think of what Boeli had said, that the Master would know about her dream. But she found, when it came right down to it, she was too shy to ask that particular question.

They sat talking in the candlelight for hours, even after the remains of dinner had been cleared away. Beauty spoke less and listened more as the evening stretched into night. Her physical weariness was taking its toll, but she did not wish to retire. It was the Beast who said at last that it was time for rest.

An involuntary sigh, half a hum, escaped Beauty's lungs. There was a moment of perfect stillness and quiet. Then the Beast rose from his chair, and Beauty followed suit.

"Beauty, will you be my wife?"

"No, my lord."

If Beauty had heard the tenderness in her own voice it would have startled her.

Her thoughts were all pleasant as she prepared for bed, and she fell asleep the moment her head touched the pillow.

Eleventh Chapter

To wake from slumber with a consciousness of well-being is to welcome joy that is knocking at your door. To be possessed of hope is to summon joy that never knocked, and is perhaps the deeper joy for not being dependent on any feeling or circumstance. Whichever type it was, Beauty did wake the following morning full of joy. It was a beautiful day; any wonderful thing could happen.

Beauty sprang out of bed and went to her wardrobe. She knew just the sort of dress she wanted to wear: a "twirly" dress, as she had called them in her childhood. She was feeling like a little girl, and was not at all ashamed of it.

She soon found a dress that perfectly suited her desire, made of a soft and light material, with plenty of fabric in the skirt for twirling. When she had put it on, she began dancing about her rooms, humming all the while.

In one of her gyrations, her hand struck squarely the vase that held her iridescent rose, sending it crashing to the floor. Her joy was arrested.

"Oh no!" She dropped to her knees and began picking up the shards. "I broke it! Oh... it was so beautiful. What a bungling oaf I am!" she chastised herself.

"It was an accident," Nasira consoled.

"Yes, but it's still broken," Beauty lamented. "At least the rose seems unharmed," she added, gently placing the flower on the table. "Is there another vase we can put it in?"

"You will find that broken things are not discarded here; it is not the Master's way," Nasira replied. "You finish gathering up the pieces, and I will show you what we will do with them."

Beauty obeyed, wondering.

When every last shard was gathered and tied safely in a large handkerchief, Nasira led her by the hand through the castle until they reached a beautiful golden door. Beyond this was a spiraling stone staircase. There were lights fixed to the wall at regular intervals as they descended. By the time they reached the bottom, Beauty was sure they must be deep underground.

Beauty could not tell much about the room that they entered; its boundaries were all in shadow, giving it a cavernous quality. A warm orange glow emanated from a giant forge in the midst of the room. The only other light was a bright lamp that hung from above, though Beauty could not discern from what exactly it was hanging. Within its circle of light was a workbench, covered with all sorts of tools for metallurgy and smithing.

"Good morning, Mehr'u'tah!" the goldsmith greeted her. "What brings you all the way down here to see me?"

Though he was invisible to her, the sound of his voice brought a vivid image into Beauty's mind. She imagined a giant of a man, with brawny arms, bare to the elbow. She imagined unruly whiskers of silvery grey covering most of his face and trailing down to his broad chest, with corresponding grey curls sticking out at odd angles from his head. Most vividly of all, she imagined his kind eyes, twinkling brightly, as though they caught and held the sparks that flew from his forge.

Beauty stepped forward, unknotted the handkerchief,

and laid it open on his workbench.

"I broke it," she said penitently.

"Hmm." He took a moment to examine the pieces. "Don't you worry, lass," he said at length. "I can mend it."

"You can?" Beauty looked up toward the origin of the voice. Suddenly she felt a giant hand against her cheek, rough with callouses, but tender in its touch.

"You leave it with me, Mehr'u'tah," the goldsmith replied.

Again Beauty had a vivid image in her mind's eye of the giant man looking down on her with paternal affection. It was as though he had lifted a burden from her shoulders that she had not known she was carrying. She felt remarkably safe and at peace.

"How long will it take to fix?" Beauty asked after a few moments of silence.

"Well, I should have all the pieces together by the end of today, but the resin that I use to join the pieces will take a fortnight to fully cure."

"Oh..." There was a note of disappointment in Beauty's voice. "As long as that?"

"There are things that cannot be rushed," the goldsmith replied. "Sometimes to hasten is to harm, and patience brings the greatest reward."

"But what am I to do with my rose in the meantime?

I do not want it to die before its vase is ready for it again. Perhaps I can put it in another vase temporarily, or even just a cup, so it has water."

"Your rose is not like an ordinary rose," Nasira interjected, "and ordinary water will do it little good. But if you take your rose every day to the enclosed garden where it grew, and dip its stem in the waters of the fountain there, it will not wilt."

"Indeed," the goldsmith remarked. "The more time you spend there, the better."

Beauty assumed he meant for the flower, that it was good for it to spend time where it grew. "I suppose there's some magic about the place," she said softly.

"Something like that," the goldsmith replied with a smile in his voice.

Beauty thanked him heartily, and said perhaps she would come see him again. "Not that I can *see* you," she added with a little laugh through her nose.

The goldsmith chuckled. "You are welcome anytime, Mehr'u'tah."

That same morning Beauty began a new routine of taking her rose to the enclosed garden, and dipping its stem in the fountain. She found it so peaceful there, and the perfumed air so refreshing, that she lingered for some time after the duty of her visit had been done. The following morning, she lingered even longer, and the morning after that, longer still. Each day she would meander around the path, noticing new buds, and watching the ever busy honey bees. Then she would sit for a while on the bench beneath the arbor, just listening. Before two weeks had passed, Beauty had become acquainted with each and every bloom, and the song of the fountain was etched in her heart.

One morning, Beauty found her vase was back in its usual place on the little table by her chair. She had not seen it since the morning that she had broken it. It was fully restored, though not identical to what it had been. Now it had seams of gold running through it, transforming the scars of its brokenness into beauty.

"It's even more beautiful than it was!" she cried in excitement.

She ran her finger along one of the golden seams, both admiring and marveling at the goldsmith's work. She peeked inside and saw that it already contained water.

"It has been filled from the fountain," Nasira

answered Beauty's unspoken question.

"I suppose there is no longer a need for me to go to the rose garden each morning," Beauty observed, with a sudden sadness at the realization.

"Perhaps for your own sake, rather than the sake of the rose," Nasira suggested.

Beauty did not catch the full meaning of this, being occupied at that moment with putting her rose into its vase, adjusting it with an artistic eye. It gave her a feeling of satisfaction to see the flower once more where it belonged. She stood a minute admiring the iridescent petals and the gold-veined porcelain.

"You know," she said suddenly, "I think I will go to the rose garden this morning after all. There is a bud I have been watching, and I want to see if it has bloomed."

After that morning, Beauty's visits to the rose garden became gradually less frequent. She was deterred by a vague feeling, whenever she was not in the rose garden, that just sitting there was a waste of time. But when she was in the rose garden, just sitting, there seemed nothing in the world more important. Once she brought a book with her, feeling a self-imposed pressure to be productive, but it only sat unopened in her lap. To be still and to listen seemed all that was required within the walls of that secret place. The fountain and the roses—the very stones of the wall—seemed to be speaking to her in a language she did not know, but if she only listened long enough, she would understand.

Twelfth Chapter

The castle was ever expanding. These words would come to Beauty's mind whenever she came across a door or staircase where she hadn't remembered one to be. But perhaps it was just her own inattention or forgetfulness after all. Perhaps they had been there all along. Nobody's memory was perfect. Could the castle really be growing? And if so, how and why? It was as much a mystery to her as when the lord of the castle had first told her of it.

Though Beauty had lived in the castle now for months, it still surprised her often. There were whole wings that were vastly different in their architectural styles and adornments than the rest of the castle. On more than one occasion, Beauty passed through a door or ascended a stair, and found herself in surroundings so different from where she had just been, that she might have thought she had passed into another country instead of another room.

One particular afternoon, Beauty came across one of those doors that she couldn't remember having seen before. It was a heavy-looking green door that came to a point at the top. It was recessed into the wall, beautifully framed by the painted mural that filled the alcove. The colors of the painting were vivid, mostly blues and greens, with just hints of gold and red.

The door opened onto a high vaulted corridor. Scalloped arches were spaced along it, with intricate openwork patterns. Detailed floral vines were etched into the walls and the ceiling, but not painted. Everything was white. Tall narrow windows, free of glass, were spaced between the arches. Sunlight streamed through them. Beauty approached one of the windows to look out, but the opening scarcely descended to her eye level. Even standing on her toes, she could see nothing but sky.

She continued slowly along the corridor, and came at length to a giant two-leaved door. It appeared to be made of polished brass. Pairs of large recessed squares went all the way up each leaf of the door. The latch was higher than Beauty's shoulder, but the hinges moved smoothly and she had no trouble, though she could feel the weight of the solid brass as the door swung open.

Beyond was a great hall with many pillars. Scalloped arches connected each pillar. Intricate geometric designs were carved into the ceiling and vividly painted in cerulean and gold. The walls and pillars were likewise covered in intricate patterns and painted vivid colors. Even the white tiled floor was covered in delicate gold detail.

Beauty found it all a bit overwhelming. She was not used to so many colors and so many patterns all at once. She wandered among the pillars, taking in the strange splendor of it all. The space was enormous.

Beyond the pillars, there were broad shallow steps going down into an open quadrangle. This roofless space was also tiled, with palms growing in stone pots around its perimeter. There was a large rectangular pool in the center, which had a tiled ledge all around it, at a convenient height for sitting. The surface of the pool was partially obscured with blooming water lilies.

Beauty sat on the ledge and looked into the pool. The light and shadow played strangely, and she thought she saw the face of a wrinkled old hag reflected in the water. A moment later she saw it was only her own face, not wrinkled and ugly. Some little fish or something living in the pool must have made ripples and distorted her reflection. She was reminded of the picture that had come alive, of the ugly old woman and the knight who loved her. She sat for a very long time staring into the pool, lost in thought, wondering about appearances, and distortions, and reality.

She brought some of these thoughts to the dinner table that evening. The Beast listened to her silly theories, now and then interjecting a single comment or question that caused her to see the whole subject from a new angle, opening her thought in a new direction.

She retired for the night with even more to think about. And the nearest she came to any conclusion was that perceptions are untrustworthy, and truth is precious.

That night Beauty had a vivid dream. Her prince was in the garden, under a tree she knew well, beckoning to her. "Come, Beauty."

The longing to answer that call was so strong it wakened her. She leaped from her bed, and rushed out into the garden, not even pausing to put a robe over her nightgown. When she reached the grassy hill where her prince had been in her dream, she was startled to a halt; sitting beneath the tree was the bulky outline of the Beast. She was about to back away slowly, when he raised his head and spoke.

"You are up early, Eysh'mehr."

"Yes..." Beauty felt terribly awkward. "I had a dream..."

"Would you care to watch the sunrise with me?"

There was a moment of silence as Beauty tried to weigh in her mind whether it would be worse to decline and walk away, or to actually sit with him.

"Yes." She came and sat by him, but not too near.

The eastern sky was already lightening, and a streak of pink and orange gradually appeared. Like a flame held to paper, the fiery colors caught the clouds above the horizon and spread.

Beauty was still puzzling over her dream. Why would she dream of her prince in this exact place, only to find the Beast here? She remembered once being warned by her dream-prince not to trust appearances. Suddenly, all the pieces seemed to fall into place. How had she not realized it before? Her heart bounded with excitement.

"Are you under a curse?" The question burst out of her.

The Beast turned toward her and their eyes met. "No; I am not cursed."

As quickly as that, Beauty's whole theory was squashed. "Oh." She looked quickly back at the eastern sky with her brow furrowed.

"I am who I am," the Beast stated.

Beauty felt ridiculous. *He is who he is,* she thought. *How foolish of me to imagine that this beast sitting beside me was really the prince of my dreams under a spell!*

The sun rose.

Like the shadows of the night disappearing in the light of the dawn, Beauty's embarrassment melted away. A feeling of perfect peace and contentment filled her as she sat there beside the Beast. It reminded her vaguely of something—of what exactly, she didn't think too hard about.

They sat for a long time in comfortable silence.

But then Beauty thought about how much time they had been sitting there in silence, and she in her nightgown.

Immediately, all the awkward feelings returned, and her enjoyment of the moment was gone. She stood, muttered something about seeing him later at dinner, and walked away quickly.

That was all very strange, she thought. *I was so sure I had uncovered the mystery at last. It would have made so much sense... But he is not cursed after all.*

Beauty returned to her rooms, eager to find distraction in almost any other subject. She went to her wardrobe and chose a dress to wear. The color of it reminded her of her sister. There was a dress of a similar color that Beauty used to have, and Mariette would tell her it was hideously out of fashion every time she wore it. Their tastes had never aligned.

This opened up a whole stream of thoughts about her family. She wondered if her sisters were well, and what Edmund was doing. She tried to calculate how long it had been since she had left them, and what time of year it must be outside of the Beast's domain. When she had arrived, it had been winter in the outside world, but early spring at the castle. Now it seemed to be late summer at the castle, so she guessed it to be spring in the outside world.

As Beauty ate her breakfast, she commented to Nasira, "Sometimes I miss my family. I wonder where they are and what they are doing, and if they are happy."

If she was honest, she missed her father and her

brother more than her sisters, but she felt guilty for this favoritism, and so lumped them all together.

"Come," Nasira replied, "I will show you something."

Nasira led her back into her bedroom, and stood her in front of the mirror that hung near her bed.

"Tap the glass twice," Nasira told her.

Beauty tapped the glass twice with her forefinger.

The reflection of her own face disappeared, and she was looking into a breakfast room, with her two sisters and her father sitting at the table. As she watched, Estella cracked her egg with her spoon, Mariette yawned, and her father took a sip from his cup. Then they disappeared, and she was looking at her brother smartly dressed, with books under his arm, stepping out of what looked to be a boarding house. He waved to an acquaintance, and then he too disappeared. Beauty was looking at her own face once more.

"How marvelous!" she exclaimed. She tapped the glass again, and saw another glimpse of the breakfast room, and the street where her brother was walking. "I can at least see that they are well, though I cannot speak to them," Beauty observed.

After this, Beauty tapped her mirror several times a day, to see what her family was doing. Some days she did this more than others.

She surmised from these glimpses that her family had left the little farm in the country. Her father and sisters appeared to be living in a large, expensively furnished house in a big, bustling city. She was quite sure the city was not Florens, but her father seemed to have reestablished himself as a merchant in this new city. As she might have guessed, her sisters were entirely absorbed in shopping, and dressing, and social engagements. Her brother appeared to have returned to university. He must have missed the first part of the term, but Beauty had no doubt he was studying hard to catch up to his peers. She had great faith in her brother's abilities.

More than a month passed in this way; Beauty keeping an eye on her family's doings, and her own days never dull. She had plenty to occupy her in the castle. Any one of the many rooms she had discovered she could revisit, each with its own attraction or amusement. Or, if the mood took her, she could venture into an unknown wing. When she felt the need for creative outlet, she had music, painting, and needlework. The gardens and grounds were always available to her for fresh air and exercise. And she could have spent several lifetimes reading and still not come close to exhausting the library.

Every evening she would dine with the lord of the castle, every evening he would ask her to be his wife, and every evening she would decline. Beauty had become so accustomed to this nightly routine, that it no longer struck her as odd.

Her conversations with the lord of the castle were always interesting, and often deep. There were moments she felt she understood him. But at other times there seemed to be an insurmountable distance between them, and she felt she could never know him. He simply could not be defined by anything within her frame of reference. No matter how hard she tried to understand him, he remained a mystery. This was a frustration, and caused her at times to subconsciously withdraw, making the perceived distance an actuality.

As time passed, Beauty saw through the mirror that her sisters both had many suitors. Mariette received all her admirers graciously, and flirted with them all equally. Estella, on the other hand, showed her favor to a certain young nobleman, whose attentions increased with this encouragement. Beauty only guessed he was a nobleman, based on his manners and dress, she couldn't tell for sure. She observed him critically, and thought he was at least less of a dandy than Sir Roger, Estella's former beau.

Edmund passed his examinations, but only returned home briefly. He signed on as a sailor aboard one of his father's ships, and set sail for some distant continent.

Beauty could only wish she knew his destination, and the duration of his voyage.

In the Beast's domain, the first touches of autumn were only just appearing in the gardens, after an unusually long summer. The evenings became quite chilly.

One morning, Beauty tapped her mirror, and saw her father sitting back in a chair with his hand on his brow, as if his head ached. She pitied him, and wished she could be there to sooth him, but never thought that it was anything serious.

The next day, it was clear her father was ill. A doctor had been summoned, and Beauty wished she could hear what he was saying. Judging by the way Mariette burst into hysterics, whatever he had said was not good news. Beauty was miserable the rest of the day, checking the mirror frequently, and worrying that no one could care for her father as well as she could herself.

Another day passed, and her father worsened. She was so distraught, she mentioned his illness at the dinner table that evening.

"I wish I could go to him," she said, never imagining that it was even a possibility. "My sisters cannot bear a sickroom. If only I were there to care for him." There was no motivation behind these words, beyond an expression of her heart's desire. She was not seeking to manipulate, or persuade.

"Will you go to him then?"

These words were so unexpected, Beauty sat silently while they slowly sunk into her brain.

"How could I?" she asked.

"If that is what you choose, I will show you how."

It was not until that moment that Beauty realized there had been a shred of something buried deep inside her all this time; it was a feeling of being trapped—held against her will. Now the truth was presented to her in its stark simplicity: she could choose.

A giddy excitement gripped her. "I may go then? Yes, please, show me how!"

The Beast gave her a gold ring with a stone that glowed like a live coal. The band was woven of three strands. It fit her finger perfectly.

"When you go to bed," the Beast instructed, "spin the ring once around your finger and say aloud where you desire to go. When you awake in the morning, you will find yourself there. You can return in the same way."

Beauty's heart was full—a strange mixture of fear for her father's health, and delight at the prospect of being a help and comfort to him. And pushing up from some deep recess of her heart, was an unexpected feeling of sadness, which she shoved down, not caring to examine.

After dinner had concluded, for the first time ever, the Beast did not ask Beauty his usual question. He only said, "Goodnight, Eysh'mehr."

Somehow, his voice communicated more to her in those few words than ever before, though he had spoken those exact words to her many times. She looked into his eyes, and saw a deep sadness there, and a deep tenderness. She knew he loved her. The sadness in her own heart swelled to the surface for a moment. There was a part of her that did not want to go away. But her father needed her.

"I will return to you soon," she said, thinking to reassure him. "As soon as my father is well. I promise."

Thirteenth Chapter

That night Beauty spun the ring around on her finger and said, "I desire to go to my father's house."

She awoke in a strange bed, in a strange room, with strange musty smells, and a strange feeling of loss in the pit of her stomach—like a hole and a lump of lead both at once. She threw off the blankets, trying also to throw off the heavy feeling.

Thick curtains covered the windows, making the room quite dark, but the faint glow that framed them, told her it was full daylight outside. She went to one of the windows, and swept aside the curtain, momentarily blinding herself with the harsh morning light that flooded in.

She was looking down from an upper-story window onto a broad paved street, with a little park opposite. The street curved in a semicircle, which allowed her to see that the house she stood in was one of a row of joined houses, all identical on the outside, making a uniform front facing the park.

She turned back into the room. Everything seemed drab and cramped; the furniture was expensive in a tasteless sort of way, and was too large for the space.

An elegant trunk sat conspicuously in the middle of the floor, looking like it didn't belong. Beauty thought it must have come with her from the castle. This was confirmed when she opened it and found dresses, shoes, and other necessary accouterments, all which suited her exactly.

Beauty dressed herself, wondering how she could explain her sudden appearance to her sisters without any fainting or hysterics ensuing. She would have liked to go to her father's room right then, and begin her tender ministrations. But of course, she did not know which room was his, and couldn't very well go poking about to find it; that seemed the likeliest way of inflicting an undesirable shock upon her family.

After some thought, she decided her best plan of action would be to break the news of her return as gradually as possible. So she slipped out of the bedroom quietly, and descended the stairs unobserved. Creeping through the house like a burglar, she successfully avoided the servants, and was soon standing in the street. She crossed over to the park and walked there for half an hour. Then she returned, and rang the bell like any visitor.

"Good morning. Is Mamselle Duveau at home?" Beauty asked the servant who answered the door.

"Yes, mamselle, but she is still at breakfast. You may leave a card."

Beauty sensed by the curtness of this reply that it was far too early for polite social calls. "I haven't any card to leave," she replied apologetically. "But I don't mind waiting. I've come from quite far. Please tell her 'Beauty has come home.' It will mean something to her."

The servant was intrigued enough by this to grudgingly show her into a sitting room.

"You may wait here, mamselle."

"Thank you," Beauty replied, but the servant was already gone.

Beauty sat and waited. Two minutes felt like ten. She

began to grow anxious. Then she heard Mariette's voice out in the hall. "What nonsense is this?" she was saying. "Beauty is dead. Lost in that wretched forest months ago."

"It must be an impostor," Estella's voice answered. "I heard gypsies often pretend to be long lost relations to get money out of you."

"Well, nothing would surprise me from a gypsy," Mariette was saying as the door opened.

Beauty stood. Her sisters entered the room. They shrieked when they saw her, and then stood staring at her with their eyes and mouths wide open.

"I heard that father was ill, so I came home," Beauty said.

"Beauty! Can it really be you?" Mariette took a step toward her.

"Yes, it's really me." Beauty took a step forward as well.

"Oh Beauty!" Estella cried, and rushed to embrace her. Soon all three were embracing and crying.

"How can this be? We thought you were dead!"

"No, I've been living at the castle with—" Beauty stopped. It didn't seem right to call him "the Beast," not when it meant something else to her than it would mean to them.

Estella and Mariette exchanged glances.

"You know, father and Edmund searched that forest for weeks after you left us and never found any trace of a castle. They had to give it up in the end. You must have had a terrible time of it, you poor thing," Mariette said in a petting tone.

"Well, actually—" Beauty began, but Estella cut her off.

"How ever did you find your way here? Did you travel alone? Have you eaten anything? There's still some breakfast left."

Beauty could see that they already questioned her sanity. If she tried telling them that she had been transported there by a magic ring, they would certainly think she was insane. So she avoided the first two questions by answering the last.

After she had eaten something, Estella took her to see their father.

"If he was more himself," Estella said in a hushed tone before they entered the sickroom, "I would say we should break the news of your return slowly, and not let him see you right away. But he's been delirious since yesterday, so I don't think he will even know you."

Beauty found her father's condition as bad as she had feared. For days, she devoted herself to his care, though he was unaware of her presence. In his delirium, he would rave about the cruel sea, and then call out Edmund's name, as though he feared the waves would take his son from him. At other times, he raved about wild beasts, fell and foul, hunting him in the dark forest. A few times he even called out Beauty's name, and then muttered incoherently about "that evil monster" who had tricked him. Beauty's concern only grew. All her father's ravings seemed full of terror and loss.

"When will Edmund return from his voyage?" Beauty asked her sisters one day.

"I only wish we knew," Estella answered. "He told us when he left that they expected the voyage to take six weeks, if the winds were favorable and their trading went smoothly, or two months, if the winds proved contrary and there were delays in their trading. It's been over a month now. So I suppose he could arrive as soon as next week, or it might be another month. Who can predict the weather?"

"I'm afraid father will never see him again."

"Oh Beauty, why must you be so morbid?" Mariette reprimanded.

That night Beauty did not sleep.

Her father tossed and turned, and moaned and muttered. And Beauty sat, and watched, and waited anxiously, wishing there was more she could do. Every so often, she bathed his head, and smoothed his pillows, but she could not fight the sickness for him.

At last the fever broke. Beauty saw her father fall into a peaceful sleep. Her relief was quickly followed by a sudden consciousness of utter exhaustion. Reluctantly acknowledging her own need for rest, she retired.

By the time her father woke, she had resumed her place at his bedside. He opened his eyes, but was slow to take in his surroundings. When his gaze rested on Beauty's face, there was a flicker of recognition. But he was too weary and disoriented to question her being there.

The next day, his eyes filled with tears when he saw her. "My little Beauty," he said weakly. "Can it be you have come home to me?"

His hand wandered over the blankets, searching for hers. Beauty gave him her hand, with tears in her own eyes. "Yes, papa, I'm here," she said.

His eyes were sunken, and his grasp was weak, but a faint smile lit his face. "Perhaps it is a dream."

"No dream, papa." Beauty shook her head. "I'm really and truly here. I've come to make you well."

His eyes closed again, but he held onto her hand. Beauty offered to read to him, but he did not respond. She thought he must have fallen back asleep, but every so often he would open his eyes to make sure she was still there, and smile when he saw that she was.

There was a marked improvement the following day, but he continued very weak.

Beauty was patiently feeding him broth in the morning, when he suddenly cast a reproving look at her.

"Where have you been all this time? You were gone for so many months. Why did you not return to us sooner?" he asked piteously.

"I have been living in the most wonderful castle," Beauty replied, "with the loveliest gardens. Don't you remember? You saw it for yourself once."

A shadow crossed her father's brow. "But we could not find any castle when we searched for you. I thought I might have imagined it all. Was there not a villainous beast who lived there?"

"Oh don't call him that," Beauty said, in real distress. "He isn't. You don't know him."

"I know he stole you from me," her father said bitterly.

Beauty did not know how to reply. She had not expected this. "Papa... I wasn't stolen. I chose to go."

"You could not return because you were a prisoner," her father said as though just remembering this fact. "But then how did you escape?"

"I was not a prisoner. There was a time when I thought I was, but I don't think I ever was in reality."

"Not a prisoner?"

"No. I was treated as the mistress of the place."

"If you could have returned to us at any time, why didn't you? You prefer the company of that beast to your own family?" There was both pain and accusation in the father's voice, and a particular note of disdain in the word "beast."

Beauty was cut by his words, more so his tone. A tear rolled down her cheek unnoticed. She didn't know how to reply, so she said nothing.

"He got tired of you, I suppose, and turned you out?" her father surmised, oblivious to the pain he inflicted. "That's the real reason you've come back, isn't it?"

"No, nothing like that." Beauty swallowed back her tears. "I wish you could understand. He's... He's not what you think."

There was a minute of silence before Beauty spoke again. "I came back because I learned you were ill, and I wanted to take care of you. I still love you, papa. That hasn't changed."

Weakened physically and mentally by his illness, Duveau's emotions were raw and volatile. Unresolved feelings rose to the surface; he felt that his own daughter had betrayed and rejected him. "Love me? Then why did you leave?" He started convulsing with suppressed sobs. "...why?"

Beauty was alarmed by this sudden escalation. "Please don't be upset, papa. You must not think about it now. You must rest." She touched her father's forehead and temple with a soothing hand. "We can talk about it when you are stronger."

She began singing an old lullaby softly, as she gathered the used dishes onto the serving tray and placed it conveniently for a servant to collect. Her father grew calmer by degrees, and eventually slipped into a light sleep. When he roused an hour or so later, he behaved as if their previous conversation had never taken place.

Duveau's convalescence was long and slow. For several days, it was as much as he could do to sit up for a few hours in the afternoons. Estella and Mariette began sitting with him during these times, though they had scarcely entered their father's room at all when he was at his worst. Mariette had said it was too depressing, and

Estella had said it only made her cry, and that that was no help at all in a sickroom. But now that he was more himself, though still very weak, they sat with him and told him all their social news.

"Now that father is well out of danger," Mariette said to Beauty one day, "you must come shopping with me tomorrow. All of your dresses are atrociously out of fashion, you poor dear."

"But I like my dresses," Beauty replied.

"Of course you do," Mariette said, trying to conceal her sneer. "But I'm afraid they are quite *inadatto*. Estella and I talked it over, and you must come with us to the soirée on Tuesday. You've been cloistered in this house ever since you returned. You must get out and be seen. And thus you must have new dresses."

Beauty complied. "I suppose we could pick out one or two."

"Wonderful! We will soon have you looking the part, Beauty."

This shopping expedition was a great trial for Beauty. She had never been particularly fond of shopping, and trying to find something that she liked that also won her sister's approbation proved exasperating for both of them. After three shops were visited, and two dresses and one hat purchased, Beauty was quite ready to go home.

But Mariette was just getting started. Beauty was dragged to five more shops, and coaxed to pick out two more dresses, as well as several accessories her sister deemed essential.

No less than four times, they ran across some acquaintance of Mariette's who was also out shopping. Each of these encounters followed a similar pattern: after exuberant greetings were exchanged, Beauty was formally introduced, and then several requisite minutes of polite conversation ensued. Beauty found these conversations tedious. They were all alike; first the flattering compliments were tossed back and forth, then the gossip was shared, and lastly, before parting, came the insincere professions of deep regard and the equally insincere wishes to meet again soon.

Beauty was quite irritable by the end of it all.

In the last shop they entered, she simply sat down near the door while Mariette flitted about like a butterfly.

"Ooh, what do you think of this hat?" Mariette held up the item in question. "The teal flowers would perfectly compliment that copper colored taffeta we got you. We could even add some copper colored ribbon. What do you think?"

"I hate it," Beauty snapped. "And I don't need another hat."

"There's no need to be an old hag about it," Mariette retorted. "You really are being ungrateful. Do you think I have done all this shopping for my own sake? No, I have done it all for you. I have only purchased one little thing for myself this whole afternoon."

"I thank you for your sacrifice." Beauty did not sound grateful in the least. "But I've said a hundred times that I just want to go home. Can we please go home? My head is aching."

"Very well," Mariette said in a saccharine tone. "Perhaps I expected too much from you on your first outing. I should have eased you in more slowly, all things considered—completely isolated for all those months! But I think we've done a good day's work."

On the drive home Mariette kept up a constant stream of chatter. "I never told you the whole story of how we came to live here in Vanitas. Well, after father returned with a solid gold chest full of precious gems, we knew we wouldn't have to live in that desolate old cottage any longer. But you know, we didn't move immediately. We stayed on for weeks while father and Edmund searched for you in that horrid forest. It was such a miserable time! By the end of it, we were quite sure we would never see you again. Really Beauty, we thought you were dead!

"But anyway, with father's wealth returned, we left

that little hovel in the country. Of course, none of us wanted to return to Florens after the way we were treated, so we came here to Vanitas, because father heard that the very best gem cutters were here. And oh Beauty, there's just no comparison! This city surpasses Florens in every way! The people here are so *elegante e raffinato.* And the food! *Non ho parole.* You can't even imagine! But you will get a taste of it for yourself at the soirée on Tuesday. And you will meet Estella's beau. He's a viscount. Very handsome, but rather serious for my taste.

"Where was I? Oh yes! Father bought this house straight away, and began trading again. He specializes in only the rarest goods, and is already well respected among the merchants of the city. We find ourselves in the highest circles of society."

Beauty was sitting with her temple resting against the cool glass of the carriage window, only half listening.

"Do sit up, Beauty," Mariette interrupted herself to say. "That posture is very unbecoming."

Beauty sat up, too mentally and emotionally drained to do anything but comply.

"You poor dear," Mariette continued in a more petting tone. "We will polish up your etiquette and deportment in no time. You must have had just a dreadful time all those months away from us. I can't even imagine what you must have been through—what horrors you endured!"

"You mean at the castle?" Beauty was paying attention now. "It wasn't at all what you think."

"You do look quite depressed," Mariette observed, thinking herself discerning, yet never considering that it was merely the strenuous day of shopping that had done her sister in. "But don't you worry, dear; we'll get your spirits up again. All of those terrible experiences are in the past now. What is that adage? Something about putting the past behind you, embracing the present, and looking forward to the future. That's what you must learn to do."

"But it wasn't a terrible experience at all," Beauty insisted. "His castle is the most wonderful place, full of beautiful and mysterious things." A wistful note had crept into Beauty's voice. "There are paintings in the gallery that sometimes come alive. And sculptures and wood-carvings that tell you stories. And strange birds that sing such beautiful songs, they make you weep. There are so many marvelous things I could tell you about, if you care to hear about them."

Mariette looked at her with a mixture of pity and confusion, which quickly melted into a patronizing smile. "Perhaps sometime, dear," she said in her most saccharine tones. Beauty could tell it was insincere.

There was a brief pause before Mariette spoke again. "Did I mention the garden party next Saturday? The Archduke is hosting, and only the elite of society are invited. We received our invitation just this morning, and the Archduke must have heard of your arrival, for you were included. You should be very honored to have such an invitation extended to you, when you have never been formally introduced to His Grace. I suppose it really reflects on Stella and me, that His Grace esteems us so highly that you were included simply by merit of familial connection.

"Oh, that reminds me! Stella and I have been discussing how we will reintroduce you into society. Of course we will take you to the theater, and the assemblies, and perhaps even the Archduke's garden party. But, you know, we must begin with the soirée and see how you do."

"I'd as soon stay home," Beauty said.

"Oh, you couldn't possibly!" Mariette exclaimed. "Not after we bought you all those dresses expressly!"

When they returned to the house, Beauty retreated to the solitude of her bedroom, and lay for an hour trying to sort her thoughts. She decided it would be best to submit to her sisters, and allow herself to be dragged along to all their parties. She would even try her best to behave according to the dictates of societal customs, though she anticipated little pleasure in it.

Another thought troubled her as she lay there: how was she going to tell her family that she would be leaving them again? They were all convinced she had returned for good. She positively dreaded broaching the subject with her father, remembering how he had reacted when they had spoken of the Beast previously. Somehow, sooner or later, she would have to do it.

But not yet. He wasn't strong yet. She would put it off till Edmund came home.

Fourteenth Chapter

Beauty's test—the soirée—was a great success in the eyes of her sisters. Enough so that they saw fit to bring her to the Archduke's garden party a few days later. This event was so much of a triumph that Beauty was miserable for days after. Her crime? Having sweet, unassuming manners, and "charming conversational skills"—that is, she listened more than she spoke. Her sentence? To sit for an hour in each of several stuffy drawing rooms, holding a cup of weak tea and pretending to enjoy dry tea cakes, whilst conversing on trivial subjects with ladies who never allowed more than three seconds of silence, until her tea was tepid, and every ladylike sip required a monumental effort not to grimace.

"You have made us quite proud, Beauty," Estella said, as they drove home from one such visit. "I don't mind saying, you have really blossomed into your name. You are already becoming quite a favorite with Lady Dalenthorp."

"If we are honest," Mariette put in, "we thought your terrible experiences would have set you back, but somehow you are more charming and graceful than before. You know, back in Florens, people used to say you were a stuck-up know-it-all, and they—"

"Mariette!" Estella scolded.

"Well, they did."

"That's not important," Estella said severely, then softened to a consoling tone as she turned to Beauty. "Never mind, dear. This is a new chapter. The past is behind you, so it doesn't matter what people thought of you or said of you back then. Everyone agrees now that you are simply the sweetest creature. You will have suitors lined up in no time."

Beauty raised her eyebrows. "Who says I want any suitors?"

Her sisters exchanged glances, which Beauty could

not interpret.

Had she really been so disliked in Florens? As she considered, she realized it was probably true. In conversation, she had listened only to judge. She had often tried to turn the subject to her own interests. Back then, she had really thought she was a selfless listener, but she had only fooled herself. A knot of confused feelings formed in her stomach. Was it the past rejection, or the self-deception that hurt the most? She couldn't tell. She was sick of all of Society's façades. Sick of all the pretentious smiles, and the idle conversation of those around her.

Beauty retreated to her room as soon as they were home. She wished she had someone in whom to confide. Her heart yearned for consolation. She thought of her dream-prince. He had comforted her more than once in her dreams. But she never dreamed of him now, not since returning to her father's house. She didn't want a dream-prince anyway. He was just another façade, not real.

She suddenly realized that she didn't want to confide in just anyone. She wanted to unburden her heart to her Beast. He would know just what to say. He would untangle the confusion of her feelings and bring clarity.

Silent tears spilled from her eyes and rolled across her face.

"I miss you," she whispered into her pillow.

In that moment, she was almost decided to return to the castle that very night.

But then she thought of her brother. They had finally heard word of Edmund, and he was to arrive the day after next. And she thought of her father. She had still not even told him of her impending departure. So she renewed her resolve to wait until Edmund had returned before using the ring.

As her father gradually recovered his strength, Beauty had begun helping him with some of his business affairs. She would organize his papers so that he could balance his accounts, and she would read aloud his correspondences and take down his replies from dictation. He grew to rely on her increasingly.

One morning they were occupied thus. Edmund was expected in just a few hours, and the father wished to get some business affairs out of the way, so that he could devote his whole attention to his son upon his arrival. Duveau had just finished dictating the last letter of business for the day, and Beauty was folding and sealing it.

"I have something I've been meaning to tell you, father," she said abruptly.

"What is it, my dear?"

"It's about the Beast, and the castle."

"I will not hear a single word about that place!" her father cried.

Beauty was stunned to silence by the vehemence of his response.

"He stole you from me, but I have you back now, and that will be the end of it," her father said decisively.

"But father, he's not what you think. If only you could understand," Beauty said desperately, her words tumbling over each other and her voice quavering with emotion. "He's good and gentle and kind."

Her father's expression changed to one of pity. "He's a monster Beauty. Whatever fantasies you created to cope with the horrors you endured, does not change the reality. Take comfort that it is all in the past now."

Beauty was mute, staring through a veil of tears. She could never make him understand.

She lowered her head and began writing the direction on the envelope she had just folded. "Just know," she said softly, "that when I disappear, I've gone back to him."

Her father pretended not to hear this speech, but it disturbed him. He began to doubt his daughter's mental stability. Was it possible she was so delusional that she would run away from home to seek her fantasy? He resolved to keep a close eye on her, and seek professional advice if things progressed.

There were several minutes of strained silence before Mariette burst into the room, full of excitement. "Come quickly! Edmund's come, he's here, he's arrived!"

Beauty started to her feet. Her father rose more slowly. Mariette rushed out again, her father following, and Beauty coming last, ready to offer her father assistance in case he grew unsteady or faint from the unwonted exertion.

They entered the vestibule. There was Edmund, with luggage at his feet, looking robust and cheerful. Mariette and Estella fluttered around him, commenting on his darkened complexion, and his growth of beard. He laughed. How Beauty had missed that sound. She watched from the doorway as Edmund saw his father approaching and stepped forward to meet him. Estella had informed her brother of their father's recent illness the moment he had set foot in the house. There was a hearty embrace between father and son. Both of them were misty eyed when they pulled away.

"I'm glad to see you, father."

"It is good to have you home, my son," the father replied.

Then Edmund caught sight of Beauty, who was still hanging back. Estella had failed to mention in her excitement the return of their youngest sister. "Beauty," he muttered in disbelief, taking half a step toward her. "Can it be?"

Beauty grinned with tears of joy springing up in her eyes. Edmund mutely spread his arms, and she ran to him. He held her for a long minute, while Estella and Mariette spoke over each other trying to explain her presence. Beauty did not bother to interrupt or correct them.

I'll tell him how it really was when we are alone, she thought.

The Duveau family spent the rest of the day sitting together, talking and listening—certain members doing most of the talking and certain other members doing most of the listening. Edmund told them about some of his adventures, and Estella and Mariette felt the need to fill him in on all the home news.

Edmund noticed Beauty's silence. He leaned towards her and put his hand on hers. "How have you been, little sister?"

But before Beauty could open her mouth, Mariette

answered for her. "She's much better now she's home, I can tell you that." And then, without pause, Mariette began talking about Beauty's recent social appearances, and how generally admired she was.

To Mariette's credit, she was speaking of Beauty as she would have wished to be spoken of herself. But all the while, Beauty sat wanting to tell her brother how she had truly been, wanting to tell him about her experiences, wanting to talk about the very subject her sister thought she was helping her to avoid.

Edmund patted Beauty's hand and gave her a look, which she understood to mean: "We'll talk later; you can tell me everything when there's no one to interrupt."

But it was several days before Beauty found an opportunity to speak to her brother alone.

The morning after his arrival, Edmund told them all, as they sat at breakfast together, that he only intended to be home for a fortnight before heading on to the university. His two older sisters immediately began planning engagements and activities, filling up what little time he had. Beauty's heart began to sink. She wondered when she would ever get the opportunity to spend time with her brother, just the two of them, like old times.

As if he read her thought, Edmund leaned over and whispered to her, "Don't worry, Beauty. I'll give them a few days, let them drag me about and show me off to their friends, and then we'll run away and find a library somewhere, just the two of us." He concluded with a wink.

Beauty smiled. She had always felt there was a deeper understanding between her and her brother than existed between her and her sisters. She longed to tell him about the castle and the Beast. But she could be patient.

It was a warm, sunshiny day when Edmund and Beauty finally found an afternoon to spend together, free to do as they pleased.

"Turns out the closest thing to a library in this house is father's study," Edmund commented. "What say we take a stroll in the park instead?"

Beauty agreed. It seemed to her that leaving the house would lessen the likelihood of interruption.

"Do you ever think about the old house in Bolanger Square?" Edmund asked as they stepped outside.

"No, not really."

"I thought you would have missed the library, and your old reading nook." He offered her his arm.

She took it. "I suppose I did when we were at the farmhouse in Isole. But it's the library at the castle that I miss now."

"Oh, right, the castle. You must tell me all about the castle." There was a patronizing note in his voice and manner, so slight that Beauty told herself she imagined it.

There was so much to tell, Beauty didn't know where to begin. So she just began telling him the first things that came to mind. She described some of the wonderful and beautiful things she had seen. She mentioned that the castle was actually growing, and there were always new rooms to discover. She told him about the invisible servants, and especially Nasira, whom she could talk to, although she could not see.

After a while, she could ignore it no longer. When she looked in her brother's eyes she could see that he was pretending; he didn't really believe her any more than her father did. Every sentence after that sounded more ridiculous, as she heard it through her brother's ears. It was no use. Beauty soon abandoned the subject.

"I wish you didn't have to leave so soon," Beauty commented after a brief pause.

"Well, I made my plans before I learned you were home." The patronizing air had disappeared. He leaned toward her in a confidential manner, "If I'm being honest, the thought of spending more than two weeks in a house with Estella and Mariette was not very appealing."

Beauty had to smile, although she shook her head at him.

"Don't worry," he said, "the term will be over before you know it, and I'll be back again to plague you. And meanwhile," he added with a mischievous glint in his eye, "I leave you in capable hands. Stella and Mary will make sure you have dozens of unsuitable suitors plaguing you constantly. And who knows? You may find a suitable one in the lot."

"I doubt it."

"Still such a pessimist."

"Why does everyone want me to find a beau, anyway?"

"It could be good for you. Turn your attention to something new. Help you live in the present. You're such an idealist."

"I'm a pessimist *and* an idealist?" Beauty asked with raised eyebrows and a wry smile.

"Yes. Somehow you are both," Edmund teased. "In fact, it is your idealism that has turned you into a pessimist, for the real world can never live up to your idyllic dreams."

"And what is your prescription, doctor?"

"Clearly, you must find a beau, and all your problems will be solved."

Beauty tried to carry on the banter, and pretend that it was just like old times, but it wasn't. There was a distance between them, which she could not define. She was left with a hollow feeling in her middle. It was like coming to the bottom of a staircase and forgetting the last step; finding no floor where you expected a floor to be.

Beauty dared not mention to Edmund that she was planning to return to the castle. He may not respond as vehemently as her father had, but she was sure he would be concerned, and very likely question her sanity. He had always been protective of her.

When they returned to the house after their stroll, Edmund ran ahead of her up the stairs, and Beauty walked past the sitting room alone. The door was slightly ajar, and she overheard Mariette's voice. Her name was mentioned and she paused to listen. Who could resist eavesdropping in such a situation?

"Poor Beauty," Mariette was saying. "You know, she was held prisoner in a remote castle somewhere—completely isolated! The monster who took her, well, I never saw him, but my father says he was hideous! Who can say what torture and abuse she endured? Anyone can see it's left her"—here Mariette dropped her voice to a dramatic whisper, enunciating each syllable with emphasis— "psychologically damaged."

"The poor dear! How terrible!" This sympathetic exclamation was from a voice Beauty did not recognize.

Then Estella's voice interjected. "She's doing much better now, I think. But I will not deny her mind is very fragile. You see, she created a fantasy utopia because she couldn't cope with the reality. That's why no one can get the truth out of her—the truth of what really happened to her all those months."

"The poor dear!" the unknown voice said again.

Beauty didn't want to hear anymore; she hurried up the stairs and shut herself in her room.

After that day, Beauty never mentioned the castle, or her experiences there, to any of her family. Likewise did she avoid any allusion to the Lord of the Castle.

The remainder of Edmund's stay sped by, and then he was gone.

It was time; she had told herself she would return after Edmund's departure.

But there was always something to make her stay another day, or another week. There was a ball she had agreed to attend. There was an acquaintance she had promised to visit. There was a concert for which her ticket had already been purchased.

Then Estella announced her engagement, and Beauty was caught up in the wedding plans. Of course Estella expected her to be a bridesmaid, and how could she disappoint her sister? So she made a new resolution: she would return to the castle after her sister's wedding.

Fifteenth Chapter

"Beauty, are you even listening?" Estella was seated at a table scattered with swatches of textile samples.

Beauty had of course not been listening. "Sorry, I was just thinking about... something else." She had been staring absently at a swatch of white and gold fabric, which she now replaced among the rest on the table. "What was the question?"

"I can't make up my mind between this lovely Aegean blue paired with the cream, or this soft sage paired with the barley. What do you think?" Estella asked, holding up the swatches in question.

"They're both very pretty," Beauty replied. "I think I prefer the blue and cream."

"Definitely the sage," Mariette said assertively. "It's so fashionable this season."

"Yes, but the Duchess's drawing rooms are all sage and gold, and I'd hate for people to think I was just mimicking her," Estella protested.

"What will it be for?" Beauty asked, totally lost.

"You really haven't been paying attention, have you? It is to be for new curtains and sofas in my drawing rooms of course," Estella replied.

"Oh! I thought we were choosing things for the wedding."

"This is for the wedding," Estella declared. "Well, indirectly. Linus agreed that we would have to redecorate both the main drawing room and the small drawing room of our new house before we move into it. Which means everything must be arranged before the wedding."

"I still say the sage," Mariette reasserted. "Just replace the barley with something pink, and then it will be nothing like the Duchess's drawing rooms. This peach blossom, for instance."

"Oh, I do like that." Estella took the pink swatch into the same hand that held the sage one.

Beauty had given her opinion, and felt that further input was unnecessary.

Lord Penninofferoy, Estella's Viscount, walked in at that moment.

"Ah, Linus dear, you can settle this for us," Estella exclaimed. "Which do you prefer for our drawing rooms?" She held up the swatches still in her hands.

He came up close to Estella's chair, and bent over it to kiss her cheek. She cocked her head to receive the kiss, and then cast him an inquisitive look. He scrutinized the textiles for a moment and then pointed decisively. "Sofas,"—and then pointing to another—"curtains."

He pulled a chair up and sat down near his fiancée.

"What about that other matter we discussed?" Estella asked eagerly with raised eyebrows. "Is everything arranged?"

"Oh yes," Linus replied. "It's all settled. Bellamy will be arriving tomorrow on the two o'clock stage."

"Beauty, I don't believe you have met Monsieur Algernon Bellamy." Estella seemed to think some explanation was necessary. "He is Linus's very good friend and will be standing up with him at the wedding."

"What say we have Bellamy around for a little dinner tomorrow," Linus proposed. His voice was oddly constrained, as though he was repeating something he had been instructed to say, or something he had rehearsed in his head. "Introduce him to your sister—both your sisters, that is. And your father."

"What a splendid idea!" Estella replied, with a purposeful nonchalance, as though trying to smooth over the stiffness of Linus's speech. "Just a small dinner party with the family. If he's not too tired after his journey, of course."

"Oh not Bellamy!" Lord Penninofferoy declared. "Journeys invigorate him rather than tire him. He's an odd bird. But an excellent fellow. The finest fellow I know. It's a wonder he's not married."

If Beauty had not been lost again in her own thoughts, her suspicions would certainly have been aroused by the significant glances Linus and Estella exchanged.

But Beauty was thinking about a dream which had disturbed her the night before. It was not a dream of her prince, but it was a dream of the Beast's castle. It was the first time she had dreamt of the castle since coming away.

In the dream, she saw the secret garden, but unlike she had ever seen it in life. The rose bushes were all bare, their leafless branches looking harsh and lifeless, as in the grip of winter. The fountain was silent.

That was all; that was the whole dream. She had

woken with a nagging feeling that it meant something, but she didn't know what.

Algernon Bellamy was well above the average height, with dark eyes, a meticulously groomed beard, and broad shoulders that were set off by a well tailored coat. These were the first things Beauty noticed about him. When he removed his hat, a fashionable mess of dark curls was revealed, rather thinning at the front.

In the half hour of drawing room conversation before dinner, Beauty also noted that his pudgy hands were prone to fidget, that his smile came easily and revealed crooked teeth, that his voice was rather louder than necessary, and that his laugh had a jarring nervous quality.

Beauty found Mssr. Bellamy was seated by her at dinner, and steeled herself to endure his conversation. To her surprise, he began straightaway upon the subject of literature, asking Beauty about her favorite authors, her favorite books, and why they were her favorites. Beauty was soon swept up in her enthusiasm over a subject so dear to her heart, and began speaking with great animation. Algernon seemed an attentive listener, and whenever she paused, he would interject another question to keep her going.

Beauty became suddenly aware that others at the table were taking note of her animation, and, she was sure, misconstruing her interest in the topic to be interest in the person with whom she was speaking. She made an effort to include others in the conversation, but to no avail. Her sisters were pleased to leave her Algernon all to herself.

Beauty resigned herself to what she could not avoid; the conversation would continue a sort of tête-à-tête. But she was determined to rein in her enthusiasm, and make him do his share of the talking. So she tried turning some of his questions back on him, wanting to know his opinions, his favorite books, and so forth. This evidently flustered him, and he tried his best to agree with whatever opinion Beauty had expressed, answering vaguely where memory failed. Beauty began to suspect that his mind had been more occupied in searching for his next question than in really considering anything she had said.

The conversation flagged.

To Beauty's relief, the company soon separated. As was proper and fashionable, the ladies retired to the drawing room, and the gentlemen remained in the dining room to enjoy a smoke and a drink.

In the drawing room, Mariette picked up some needlework to occupy her fingers. Estella sat herself at the harp, plucking a few chords, but doubtless waiting for Lord Penninofferoy to enter before performing a song. Beauty sat, staring absently at a candelabra. It was many minutes before anyone spoke.

"You seemed to enjoy the company of Monsieur Bellamy," Estella said suddenly to Beauty, who glanced up in time to catch her sister's meaning smile.

"I enjoyed the subject more than the company," Beauty replied composedly.

"I told you bookish talk was the way!" Mariette said triumphantly.

"What do you mean?" Beauty asked, with mounting suspicions.

Estella gave Mariette a warning glance, which she failed to notice.

"We told him books were the way to your—" Mariette stopped suddenly, realizing her mistake too late.

Beauty raised her eyebrows. "The way to my...?"

"Oh, it doesn't matter," Mariette said quickly. "We knew you wouldn't give him a chance unless he had some edge."

"I see," Beauty said. So, Algernon Bellamy had been schooled on how to speak to her, on which topics to pursue, and likely which to avoid. Beauty felt tricked. Not that it mattered much. Even with such instruction Beauty had ultimately found his conversation wanting.

"You're not upset, are you?" Estella asked.

"No, I'm not upset," Beauty replied. "I know you meant well by it."

Mariette sighed with relief. "I thought sure you would be angry if you found out we'd set it up."

"Does *he* know you set it up?" Beauty asked.

"Oh yes! He came down a week earlier than originally planned just to meet you."

"That's a bit unfair, him knowing and me in the dark," Beauty said, but she was smiling. The humor of it all had struck her.

"He really is a fine fellow, Beauty," Estella declared, encouraged by Beauty's calm demeanor to press the suit. "Even if he isn't as well-read as you. And he's got the kindest, most generous heart!"

"Indeed," Mariette concurred. "Do give him a chance. He may surprise you."

"I suppose he may," Beauty assented, bent on avoiding further discussion of the subject.

They heard the gentlemen approaching not long after.

Estella began her song, plucking the harp strings with more elegance than skill. Mssr. Duveau, upon entering, picked up a book and retired to a corner of the room. Lord Penninofferoy placed himself near his fiancée. And, though Beauty carefully avoided eye contact, Bellamy soon came to sit near her, hoping to rekindle their dead conversation.

He had not been seated half a minute before Beauty was forced to admit to herself that Mariette had been right: Algernon Bellamy had surprised her. It was as though he had hit his head, and all memory of their conversation at dinner had been knocked out of his brain. He did not merely return to the topic, he repeated the very same questions.

Haven't we been over this? Beauty thought, bemused. *He really wasn't paying attention at all.*

She determined not to make it easy for him, though she felt herself mean in doing so. She began voicing opinions that were not her own, quite contrary to those opinions she had voiced at the dinner table. Poor Algernon did not seem to notice.

Beauty entertained herself in this way for what remained of the evening, contradicting herself to see if he would perceive it. He invariably agreed with whatever she said.

At last, Bellamy left with Lord Penninofferoy. Beauty was glad when they had gone.

Mariette intercepted her on the stairs. "Well?" she asked eagerly.

"I don't like him," Beauty said flatly. *He's an absolute fool,* she added to herself.

"How can you say that after one evening's acquaintance?" Mariette cried. "Beauty, dear, don't steel yourself against him so quickly. You are always so quick to judge, and so sure of your judgments."

Mariette retired to her room, never guessing how her words would sink into her sister's mind; how they would goad her one step further down a path of thought that Another had first set her on.

Long did Beauty lie awake thinking.

So sure of your judgments.

How was it that even after realizing her sight was dim, and her judgments fallible, she still trusted in them so much? How was it that after feeling so acutely the misjudgments of others toward herself, she still judged so mercilessly? How could she be so hypocritical?

She thought of the Lord of the Castle—his gentleness and patience. Who knew better than he what it meant to be misjudged and misunderstood?

She suddenly thought of something Nasira had once

said to her:

"If I were to give you an answer, then you would think that you knew the answer, and it would only delay your true understanding."

Truth was not a packaged commodity; one could not receive it, open it, and keep it stowed by for when it was useful. It was rather more like flowing waters, Beauty thought, and she was the riverbed, with rocks and dirt, twigs and dead leaves, choking what ought to be a wide river into a shallow and narrow streamlet. Her capacity for the Truth was limited. It was a thought that grieved her. If only the sediment and stone and lifeless debris could be cleared away, then her capacity would increase and she would flow more deeply. She fell asleep with this thought in her mind, not knowing that a great stone had indeed been cleared away.

When she awoke the next morning, she had a distinct feeling that she had dreamt of her Beast and his castle, but she was unable to remember a single particular of the dream. She found this vaguely frustrating. All she knew was that the color and vibrancy in the dream made the waking world seem pale and lackluster.

The days passed one after another, full of various activities which others had planned. During the day, Beauty found temporary diversion in these activities, forgetting for a time her deeper discontent. But in the evenings, alone in her room, she felt desolate and unhappy.

Many times she came very near spinning the ring around on her finger, but each time something stopped her.

Did she not have a duty to her family?

It was only right that she stay for her sister's wedding.

More and more often Beauty would wake in the mornings with the feeling—sometimes only a vague suspicion, sometimes almost a certainty—that she had dreamt of her Beast, but unable to remember anything of her dream. In those first minutes after waking, her thoughts would dwell in the Beast's domain. But then the duties of the day would invade her mind, and such thoughts were pushed aside.

Algernon Bellamy made several more attempts to court Beauty after their first meeting. He was slow to discern her disinterest, and for this Beauty was partially to blame. Feeling guilty for her harsh and hasty judgments, she perhaps overcompensated at their next encounter; even a modest man might have misconstrued her friendliness. But quite suddenly, some days before the wedding, he began ignoring and avoiding her. Beauty could only guess by this that he had given up the suit. And she was glad of it.

The day of the wedding dawned at last. It was a grand occasion; everything Estella could have wished. She felt herself a very queen of Society. Adorned in costly silks and pearls, she was declared "the most beautiful bride that ever was," and the bridegroom was declared "the luckiest man alive."

Beauty suffered most of the day in a fashionable dress of her sister's choosing, which pinched her under the arms and impeded the proper operation of her lungs. But she smiled and laughed and danced, as was expected of her, and found solace in the fact that everyone else seemed very happy.

The feasting and revelry lasted far into the evening, and the tongues of Society chattered on about the grand wedding of Estella Duveau to Lord Linus Penninofferoy for weeks to follow.

Sixteenth Chapter

Beauty at last found herself alone in her room in her father's house, breathing freely in a ruffled nightgown, the offending bridesmaid dress draped over a chair. She crawled into the bed, blew out the candle, and lay back against the pillows with a sigh. Her body was exhausted after the constant activity of recent days, but her mind was wide awake.

Three days before, Beauty had awoken filled with a strange joy and excitement, knowing she had dreamt of the Castle and the Beast. She was unable to remember the particulars of the dream, but the fingerprints of it were in her mind. Though the dream was gone, there was a phrase that lingered behind: *deep unto deep.* It no longer seemed grievous to her that she had only scratched the surface of so many truths she used to think she knew; it was now a delight that so much beauty and depth she had still to discover.

The next night, she had dreamt of her iridescent rose, in its blue and white vase with the golden seams where it had broken and been restored. But the flower was wilting; all its petals drooped toward the ground, as though weighed down by some burden too heavy for them.

The following night, Beauty had again dreamt of her rose wilting, looking a picture of sadness. But in the morning, she had pushed it from her mind, for it had been the day before the wedding and there had been much to do.

That night, for a third time, she had dreamt of her rose. Its drooping petals looked dull, their iridescence faded. But the morning brought Estella's wedding day, so she had once more pushed the dreams from her mind.

Now she lay awake, staring up into the darkness. The wedding was over. The time had come at last to return. She touched the ring on her finger, but did not spin it.

She began imagining the aftermath of her

disappearance. It would be the second time her family would lose her. How could she do that to them? Perhaps she ought to stay just as long as Edmund was in town. That was only a few more days.

No.

She must leave now. She had already delayed so long, stretching weeks into months. There would always be some reason for her to stay—something to keep her. Mariette would get married. Edmund would graduate. Estella would have a baby. If she didn't return now, who could say how long the next delay might prove to be?

Now was the time.

She ran her forefinger along the woven bands of her ring, and across the facets of the fiery gemstone.

Oh, why was it so hard? She longed to return to the castle. So what was preventing her?

Her family had some hold on her; she felt she owed them something. Was not that right and proper? Was not that the part of a loving and dutiful daughter?

Somehow it was easier to continue on, day to day, in this life her family had built, empty and unsatisfying though it was, rather than make the decisive step to leave.

But her heart ached for her home, and this place was not her home.

She remembered his eyes, when her Beast had said

"Eysh'mehr" the last time. He did not only love her, but *knew* her. The longing was stirred up afresh in her to know him and uncover all the mysteries that shrouded him and his castle.

Her heart was set. She spun the ring around on her finger and whispered aloud into the darkness. "I desire to return to my King and his Kingdom."

Never before had she consciously thought of him as a King, but now she spoke from her heart, and her heart had known it. She drifted off to sleep marveling that she had never thought of it before. Of course he was a King. Not a lord merely, but a lord of lords. She marveled, too, as she realized that that was what "Beast" had come to mean to her.

The moment Beauty regained consciousness, she sat up and looked about her expectantly. There was her own little gilt clock, with its sweet tones telling the hour. And on a little table by her bed was her own rose, blooming as ever in its beautiful vase, its petals flashing with rainbows in the soft morning light.

At the foot of her bed was standing a beautiful woman, with silver hair flowing down her back and a gentle countenance. She looked both old and young, and when she moved, her hair shimmered like moonlight on a lake.

"Nasira!" Beauty cried, recognizing the servant instantly. "I'm home!" It did not seem strange to her that she could see Nasira for the first time. Her thought ran swiftly to the desire of her heart, and she asked without pause, "Where is he?"

"Seek in the garden; you will find him there." Nasira's smile shone out through her eyes.

Beauty sprang from her bed without a second thought. Into the gardens she ran in her nightgown, out through the green tunnel, past the purple and yellow flowers. The sun shone warm on her skin. A gentle breeze whispered among the branches of new-budding trees. Fountains babbled joyously, and flowers bloomed everywhere. For a quarter of an hour Beauty walked up and down the pathways eagerly searching. Then it dawned on her: *the* garden. The secret garden. She turned her steps thitherward.

Her pace slowed as she approached the archway. She stopped beneath the green vines with their small blue flowers. There he was, standing beside the singing fountain, blooming roses all around. He had the shaggy black coat of a bear, the horns of a ram, the fangs and claws of a lion. He was somehow both more terrifying and less terrifying than she had remembered him. For a fleeting moment she feared his wrath. Perhaps he would be angry that she had delayed so long in returning.

She looked into his eyes, and was held captive by them. They were like deep wellsprings, and like burning flames. She was filled with regret for having stayed away so long. But that, too, was fleeting. The love in his eyes was overwhelming, and melted away both fear and regret.

"My Beast," Beauty whispered. She stepped forward, and suddenly found herself in his arms, pressed to his heart. She had never felt more safe. It reminded her of her dream-prince. But that had only been a shadow; this was the reality. Time lost all meaning. It could have been minutes or hours that Beauty rested in his embrace. She was perfectly content, and had no inclination to move.

Suddenly, she heard his voice in her ear. "I will see you at dinner."

Then he was gone.

She opened her eyes, and she was standing alone by the fountain.

Beauty returned to her rooms. She had a long conversation with Nasira, while she dressed and ate breakfast.

It was good to be home.

She spent the whole of that afternoon visiting all the beloved places she had missed: the library, the aviary, the music room, and a dozen others.

Finally it was time to dress for dinner.

As Beauty looked through her wardrobe, she was mysteriously drawn to a deep red dress, with an intricate pattern of tiny white flowers embroidered into the front of the bodice, and around the bottom of the skirt. Nasira helped her into it, and then sat her down to arrange her hair.

"I think this will suit," Nasira said, as she placed a woven crown of small white flowers like miniature lilies upon Beauty's head.

Beauty looked at her reflection and smiled with delight. "They're beautiful," she said, meaning the flowers.

There was a knock on her door.

A smartly dressed servant entered holding a candelabra.

"It's you!" Beauty cried before he could speak. "The floating candelabra!"

A shadow of a smile appeared briefly at the corners of his mouth, but he said quite stoically, "Dinner is served, Mehr'u'tah."

As Beauty followed him down the corridor, she asked, "What's your name? I can't just call you 'the holder of the candelabra'."

"You could," he replied impassively. "Or you could call me Eldon."

"How are you this evening, Eldon?" Beauty asked.

"Quite well, thank you for asking."

They entered the grand dining hall. To Beauty's eye everything looked at once familiar and new. The great chandelier of crystal and gold seemed even larger than she remembered. The blue and green curtains seemed more exquisite, the carvings on the walls and pillars more intricate.

And there was the King awaiting her. Once more she felt that he was both more terrifying and less terrifying than she had recalled.

Beauty approached him and curtsied low before him. "My lord," she said, and then her smile beamed up at him as she raised her bowed head. If her sisters had seen her then, they would have been struck speechless by the regal elegance of her manner and movements. But Beauty wasn't thinking of herself at all.

Servants brought in the first course. And then the second course, and the third. And Beauty talked, with her heart open, like a sunflower to the sun. And she listened, like one drinks who finds a spring in a desert place. To Beauty, it seemed they had just sat down, when the third course was cleared away, and the fourth laid before them: a filet of fish, from which issued the rich smells of browned butter and the sharper smells of herbs and lemon.

"I was just thinking," Beauty commented before taking her first bite of fish. "The castle has been growing in my absence. There must be so many rooms I haven't seen."

"Indeed," the King replied. "And outside the castle, too, there is much you have yet to discover. You have not seen the wild horses of the south pasture. Nor have you sailed upon the waters of the Deep Lake. Nor climbed the great mountain to feed the goats. Nor traversed the caverns beneath the mountains to see their many wonders."

"I want to do all of those things!"

"So you shall."

Before Beauty thought it possible, considering she was doing more talking than eating, the seventh and final course had been cleared away.

"I have so many names for you now," Beauty remarked. "My lord, my savior, my king. And still, none of them seem to do you justice."

"It is good, for no one name could define me. I am myself. That is all. Do you want to know my favorite name that you have given me?" he asked with a twinkle in his eye.

"What name?" Beauty asked, but she blushed, already suspecting.

"Beast," came the answer. "For that is the name you have allowed me to define; the others you have used in your attempts to define me."

"You remind me of something Nasira once said to me. I had not understood it then, but I understand it now—well, that is, I understand it a little better now. Perhaps six months hence I will look back to this moment and say, 'I did not understand it then'."

The Beast only smiled.

There was a long silence, which Beauty broke at last. "I had forgotten how wonderful it is just to sit in the company of one you trust." She looked about the room. The fire had been allowed to die down to glowing embers, but the candles were well trimmed and burning brightly. She turned again to the Beast. "I suppose I had better retire. There is so much I want to do tomorrow."

The Beast rose without a word. Beauty stood also. She knew what was coming.

"Beauty." He looked down at her with eyes full of love. "Eysh'mehr," he spoke slowly, "will you be my wife?"

Beauty's heart thrilled. She looked him full in the face. "Yes, I will, my beloved Beast."

There was a flash of light that blinded her, and a rumbling boom like thunder. When her eyes adjusted, there was no longer a beast standing before her. It was the form of a man, but larger and more powerful than any man Beauty had ever seen. The light that had blinded her was emanating from him; his face was radiant. Somehow he was even more terrifying in this form. If she had felt herself to be his enemy, she was sure she would have melted into a puddle of fear at his feet. Even knowing herself to be his beloved, she sank down to her knees before him. There were sounds of trumpets and celebration, but it was all too much for her brain to process.

"I don't understand," Beauty cried when she could find her voice. "You said you were not cursed!"

"Nor am I," the King replied. "I have not changed. I am as ever I was. It is your eyes that have been renewed."

"I was cursed?" Beauty asked in wonder.

"In a way." He raised her gently to stand before him.

That's when she noticed her dress had changed from dark red to pure white. It was the same dress, with the same flowers embroidered over it, but the color had all gone out of it. Suddenly she laughed, joy overtaking her wonder. "I seem fit for a wedding."

"You are my Bride." The King took her in his arms, as he had done in the garden.

"My own dear Beast," Beauty whispered into his chest. "How much I have still to learn about you."

And so it began; humility had paved the way, and love had opened the door.

ABOUT THE AUTHOR

Bethany Kohler

Reading is the best teacher of writing. Bethany grew up in a large family with no television, plenty of books, and a big backyard where she "played pretend" with her brothers.

As an introverted adolescent, she counted many fictional characters among her friends, and many dead authors among her mentors.

Her interests have always tended toward the artistic and domestic; in addition to reading and writing, her pastimes include drawing, singing, sewing, and crafting. She earned her Culinary Arts Degree in 2012, and enjoys cooking and baking for friends and family. She has also worked for many years as a nanny, and loves spending time with the children of her siblings, cousins, and friends.

www.ingramcontent.com/pod-product-compliance
Lightning Source LLC
Chambersburg PA
CBHW031951170626
46807CB00006B/2437